# BAT AND THE BLITZ

## A FUC ACADEMY STORY

### A. GREGORY

# ACKNOWLEDGMENTS

As always, my main dude/husband gets a tip of the Santa hat. It is honestly impossible to explain how wonderfully supportive this man is. You're definitely the perfect man for me, baby! I love you forever and a day. Thanks for being my guy, for being by my side... or pushing me up that hill when I need a boost.

A huge thanks to Eve for allowing me to write in her world for the second time this year. Also, thanks for letting me add Santa Claus in FUC. Never thought I'd say those words in my life, but I'm sure glad I did!

Another huge thanks goes to Jessica Ripley who gets things done! You're a badass lady with Yoda-esque energy.

To Devin Govaere, thanks for making my book baby all clean. You're the best! Thanks for reading a Christmas novella in the middle of summer.

And of course, a huge thank you goes to you, dear reader. I hope you enjoyed Raya and Klaus... err, I mean *Blitz's* story. ;)

*For my husband,*

1

———

**RAYA**

*Deep breath in. Deep breath out.*

I force a few more gulps of air into my lungs, but I'm not calmer.

If anything, with every puff, I'm more agitated.

It's got nothing to do with the air quality in the house and everything to do with my sister's stifling presence. Poor Vera doesn't even *know* she drives me nutso bananas. But she does.

I suppose it's a typical way for little sisters to feel about their *perfect* big sisters.

This is way more intense, though.

We passed good old sibling rivalry a decade ago. Maybe even two.

Not that the competition between us is fair *or* right.

There's no contest. I've never had a chance of winning. Not against Perfect Vera. My sister's only flaw is that she cannot stand the sight of blood. It was the one thing I could do better: be a vampire bat. I leaned on it *hard* growing up.

When I got a bad grade—rather, when I got a *lower* grade than the standard Little Miss Perfect set up—it was much easier for me to cope with my parents' disappoint-ment if they were *also* let down by Vera's inability to drink blood.

Is that nice? No.

It's petty as hell, but a bat's *gotta* do what a bat's *gotta* do.

It's basically the only way I survived in my high-achieving family. It's not my fault I don't have the kind of brain that *wants* to sit around and read a whole bunch of theories and write long briefs or do long math equations.

*Yuck.*

Sitting still is not my jam. I much prefer action.

That's why I applied to the Furry United Coalition Newbie Academy. I was basically killing my soul, trying to complete a university degree in criminology.

It was interesting enough, but a three-hour-long lecture?

No, fucking *thank* you.

I didn't know how to be motionless for that long. I went on so many panic flights halfway through those inter-minable classes I had to drop it from my schedule.

After discussing this with my older and *very* wise cousin Mila, she suggested that I apply to FUCN'A. As a forensic anthropologist and sometimes teacher at the Academy, Mila was in a great position to tell me what to expect. She helped me along the application process in secret. I figured I'd only break the news to my parents once I was accepted. It was the responsible thing to do, but it was also self-preservation.

If they didn't know I applied, *if* I failed, they wouldn't need to know.

Of course, it wasn't that easy.

Before I even got into the Academy—before I could tell my family I had applied—Vera announced that she was leaving her job as a fancy lawyer to join FUCN'A.

That's right.

Read that three times over, and don't you dare judge me for going a little nutso bananas. I got a cool Bela Lugosi tattoo out of *that* major freak-out, so I suppose it could've been much worse.

Without telling anyone, least of all me, Vera got into the Academy.

I *almost* withdrew my application when I found out, but Mila convinced me to give it a shot anyway.

"Who cares if it *might* look like you were merely following behind Vera? You made the decision *long* before she announced she had been accepted. *You* know, and that's all that matters." Mila's words were comforting enough in the moment, but they're little comfort right now.

Vera graduated from FUCN'A ahead of me after one hell of a first mission. Not to say that the competition between us is more aggressive than ever, but it sort of is. How can I prove myself better than her now?

Simple.

I can't.

I can't even lord Vera's aversion to blood over her anymore.

All because of that silly pumpkin head scientist boyfriend of hers. Vera doesn't even *need* to drink blood to survive anymore. Jack made her some kind of plant-based supplement.

I would be pissed off if it wasn't so damn sweet.

I love my sister. I do. I don't want to see her fail, nor do I wish her a miserable life. I like her fine, but she'd be a hell of a lot more likable if she wasn't so damn good at Every. Little. Fucking. Thing.

Even the dish she brought over to Mila and T-Bone's place for our potluck dinner is better than the store-bought dessert I grabbed. Did I spend hours making something?

No. Instead, I hit the gym. I don't regret my choice, but my brain can't help but compare Vera and me.

It's basically how my brain is wired.

In fact, I'm so caught up in my own damn thoughts I lose track of the conversation.

Tuning back in, it takes me a few moments to realize Mila is trying to pry information out of Vera about her latest assignment, namely tracking a woman who was either the mastermind in Vitality Holdings' whole immortality quest or a victim of the shadowy and unknown leaders, Hera and Zeus.

"You're on my husband's task force," our cousin Mila grunts, wrangling her squirming baby into her arms. "You can tell me *everything*. I'll claim that T-Bone told me during pillow talk."

Vera blushes deep. "Oh, no. You know I can't. I'm not at liberty to divulge anything I've learned during my stakeouts of Lisbeth Bannon." She sighs dramatically like she doesn't absolutely *adore* having sensitive information.

Mila clicks her tongue. "I'm on maternity leave. Bored out of my skull. Give me something. An exciting tidbit. I beg of you."

Tiny little Bettina coos up at her mother, and immediately, Mila, the badass, melts away. Her gaze brims with love as she grins down at her offspring. "You're the cutest baby bat *ever*, Bettina Thrussel. Yes. You are."

My sister smirks at me. It's the kind of conspiratorial look siblings give each other, and I *almost* don't return it. I do, though. Because if there is one amusing thing in life, it's that Mila Starling, the daughter of the infamous prolific serial killer known as the Bloody Doctor, has a daughter of her own.

Before Bettina was born, I never would've guessed that

Mila would settle down and have kids. But, seeing her holding her kid, big moon eyes shining with happiness, it's clear that my cousin is batshit in love with her child.

Oh, Mila still rocks really funny, albeit borderline-inappropriate shirts and her firetruck red hair. She's also one of the best moms out there. She literally knows *exactly* what *not* to do.

Like don't kill hundreds of people to learn the secret of immortality.

That's hardly a good way to do some mother-daughter bonding.

"Did you hear that? I think Jack is calling me." Vera hastens to the kitchen, undoubtedly uncomfortable with the thought that she couldn't fulfill Mila's desire for information.

As soon as my sister disappears into the kitchen, Mila switches seats and comes to sit beside me. "Okay, sour bat. Tell me what's wrong," she commands, bouncing a gurgling Bettina.

"I'm fine." I'm not, but I'm not going to unload on Mila. She's got a screaming bundle of joy to tend to. I'm not going to pile on my drama. It wouldn't be right.

"You're not *fine*. I can see that vein in your temple about ready to explode." Mila holds Bettina with one arm to poke at the vein that is indeed popping out of my temple.

I *hate* that it does that. It's one of the reasons why I always leave my hair down and wavy. It hides The Vein. It's no fun having a clear physiological sign that tells people *exactly* how you're feeling. It gives them an unfair advantage.

Knocking Mila's hand out of the way, I tug at the lapels of my leather jacket. "I'm just waiting for my first mission right now. I'm antsy."

Mila gives me a knowing look. "This is about the task force."

"Shh." I crane my neck to look toward the kitchen, but Vera is out of earshot, talking with T-Bone and Jack.

"Oh, come on, Raya. It's not so bad. I'm sure you'll find a way to leave your mark on the Academy."

I snort hard. "Sure. Because lightning strikes twice in the same family."

She shrugs. "It does in ours. Think about it. When my mom escaped from prison, I was pulled into the mission to bring her in. We all thought that would be the end of the Bloody Doctor and her super-nasty research. Then? Your sister is sent to be Jack's bodyguard. *Boom.* He's involved in a whole thing with sketchy people who want the key to immortality, too. There's a whole task force dedicated to finding anything and everything we can about any and all immortality chasers out there. If you want, I can ask T to pull you into one of the teams."

I shake my head. "Not a chance."

"Stop being like that. You could do some good out there. You know all about the Bloody Doctor *and* this whole Vitality Holdings, Lisbeth Bannon, Hera and Zeus thing your sister uncovered."

"Well, sure. Because of *course* my sister would discover this huge plot to take over the world during her first mission."

Mila waves me off. "Point is that *you* have a chance to be part of the task force, too. You could even uncover the real identity of Hera and Zeus while your sister is tailing Lisbeth Bannon."

Her words don't sit well with me. In fact, I get the distinct impression that she is keeping something from me. I narrow my eyes at her, pursing my lips as I read her face.

Her brows are puckered together with a tiny bit of stress. There's a slight edge of panic wafting off of her that has nothing to do with the baby in her lap.

I gasp and hit a hand to my knee. "No fucking way."

"Don't yell," she chides. "You'll scare Bettina."

The child hasn't budged. She's still sitting there, looking as pleased as the queen of everything, as cute as a button.

"Why do I get the feeling you're trying to warn me about something? If you tell me T-Bone asked Director Cooper to put me on the immortality chasers task force, I'm gonna make ground beef out of your husband."

Mila laughs. "Sweet mother of echoes. T didn't *request* you. Alyce gave him a list of agents to assign to the task force. Your name was on it with an asterisk. The boss lady wants you on this. That's a huge compliment."

The bottom falls out of my stomach, and the blood I had for lunch races back up to burn the back of my throat. "No."

Her apologetic smile twinges. "This is good. It's a good assignment for you."

I inhale long and deep, my hands fisting at my sides.

I should've known that I would be in Vera's shadow in FUC, too.

How in the hell can I make a name for myself now?

## 2

# KLAUS

*You've got to be fucking joking.*

I try to keep my body still, but my legs are itching, developing a mind of their own. Hell, even my fingers are twitching. Every single particle of my body is vibrating with barely contained annoyance, right down to the hair in my beard. With all of the professionalism I can muster, I clear my throat and run a hand back through my shoulder-length hair. I pull hard when my fingers hit a tangle, but the pain offers no relief from T-Bone's words.

"I'm not sure I understand," I say through *almost* unclenched teeth, leaning back against the chair.

Agent T-Bone Thrussel, a Highland cattle shifter a few years older than me, leans back in his own seat with a sigh. He's almost as tall and built as me.

Even his beard wants to rival mine.

Yet, we are as similar as we are different.

Where T-Bone has a beard, clean-cut hair, and a buttoned-up attitude that *screams* Type A anal-retentive, I'm a tatted-up, long-haired motorcycle-owning, rule-breaking agent.

That's probably why T-Bone has something I don't have: a position of authority.

Not that I would *ever* want to be in his shoes. The man left the RCMP to work with the Furry United Coalition a little while ago. He's already heading up his very own—and brand-new—task force. He's quite literally a golden boy. Not only because of his blond hair but because Director Cooper seems to have a soft spot for him.

That means pissing T-Bone off will only get me into a shouting match with the boss lady.

I don't want that. Not again. Not so soon after the little hiccup on my last mission. I'm on thin ice with Director Cooper, but what else is new? She was aware of what she was getting when she hired me. I've never claimed to be a team player, patient, or even law-abiding.

T-Bone shakes his head when I ask for more clarification. "Look, Klaus. I know you've got this whole loner thing going for you. You don't like working with a partner, and I get it. I do. This isn't negotiable, however. What's going on in the world right now is too important to be left up to only *one* person."

I bite down hard on my teeth. T-Bone might *say* he gets it, but he doesn't.

No one does.

I don't merely *hate* working with a partner. I *can't*.

Sitting around to discuss strategies and taking the time to let someone else in on my plans and theories takes way too damn long.

Too much wasted energy sitting around blabbering. Not enough action.

"I'm sure if you tell me what the mission is, I can set your mind at ease that I can do it alone."

*Talk, talkety-talk. Just some useless words, wasting precious time.*

T-Bone doesn't appear remotely convinced. He huffs out a breath and rubs a hand across his beard. "Not a chance. I chose you specifically for this mission because of your no-nonsense attitude. We need it in this case. I can't send someone who will be roped into the celebrity and magic of it all. Besides, you have an advantage here."

I have no idea what that means, but it doesn't matter. I don't work with a partner. Forget those harried detectives in the movies who don't work well with others because they're the loose cannons. I'm *not* the loose cannon. It's the partners I've been given over my career who are sketchy and inconsistent. Each one is denser than the last.

"T-Bone, let me assure you. Me working with someone else will only make things complicated."

"No, this is too important for one person."

It's my turn to arch a brow, but I don't insist anymore. The man is a second away from calling the director. I can *feel* his impatience down to the marrow of my bones.

"You're going up north to protect Santa Claus." T-Bone delivers the assignment like he's delivering a death sentence. Not a joke. His face is stern and worried, which is the *only* indication that this might not actually *be* a joke.

I chuckle, nervous for the first time in a long time. "I don't get it."

*This cannot be real. This* isn't *happening.*

"You know what I'm saying, Klaus. Don't make me elaborate."

"You can't be serious."

T-Bone gets to his feet and begins pacing his office. "I don't need to tell you that up in the very north of the country, there is a small village. It's fly-in only unless you have a sleigh. It's Christmas Town. *The* Christmas Town. Santa lives there with his elves. The townspeople all have jobs in the toy industry, too."

He's got to know that I'm all too familiar with this. The only person in the world who knows *who* I am and *where* I come from is Director Alyce Cooper. I'm getting the serious impression that T-Bone knows now, too.

I cross my arms to keep from bouncing out of my chair and quitting my job. I've had a good run working for FUC. I can quit. Go do something else where no one knows my history.

That's not exactly right, though.

I'm not qualified for much of anything else.

"I'm sure you're aware of that legend." T-Bone's eyes plead with me to jump in.

I don't. I *really* don't want to have this conversation.

T-Bone winces at my silence but goes on. "A long time ago, an adventurer supposedly found the Holy Grail."

I blink at him before snorting dryly as he continues.

"The Holy Grail. Just like in Indiana Jones and the Arthurian tales. This chalice is a sacred relic that dates back to pre-Christian times. Of course, *they* took the myth and ran with it. This cup is said to be forged in a blessed and hallowed metal that gives the drinker immortality."

I'm not simply frowning. I'm downright glaring at T-Bone. I don't appreciate the joke, but I'm seriously waiting for him to start laughing.

The man needs a better sense of humor, or I need one, full-stop.

"A legend states that the Holy Grail was melted into a gold wreath and kept in Christmas Town. It gives the village and Santa their magic, or so it's believed. The wreath has always been safe up there. It's so cold and so remote the tale barely made it to the general public."

I open my mouth to comment but snap it shut. I literally have no comeback for this. Besides, the more I say, the lower my chances are of talking my way out of this.

"We can't let anyone get their hands on that wreath. Whether the fable is true or not doesn't matter. No one wants Vitality Holdings to find it."

"Still not sure what the hell this has to do with me," I lie.

"Ever since the Bloody Doctor's research was posted online by her maniacal sidekick Oscar Trow, there has been an increase in immortality chasers. First, it was with the Bloody Doctor's blood work. These people thought they could use blood to live forever. Then, a few months ago, they moved on. They tried to prove immortality could be found in shifter and plant genome."

Right. I'd heard about that. One of the newly minted agents was sent to babysit a scientist, and the next thing they knew, the mad botanist turned into a pumpkin. The damn thing grew legs and arms. It was a damn nightmare to witness. The evil plot to use plants to live forever found a way to infiltrate the Cryptozoian Council. One of the agents there was being blackmailed.

A pair of lunatics, calling themselves Hera and Zeus, injected the agent with a toxin that would kill her unless she had an antidote every day. So long as she listened to the instructions given to her by her blackmailers, she would remain alive.

Silence and cooperation for her life.

That was the bargain.

It's hard to believe. I wouldn't have gone for it. At all. You couldn't pay me enough to make me betray FUC.

Even if that payment was my own damn life.

"You're gonna be heading up to Christmas Town with

Agent Raya Slaski. Your mission is to guard the wreath and make sure no one steals it."

I burst out laughing.

How could I not? This was a joke. It *had* to be.

"What's so funny?" T-Bone asks, frowning deep.

"You just told me you want me to go back to *Christmas Town* to guard the wreath and to keep Santa safe."

T-Bone shook his head. "You're making it sound really ridiculous."

"'Cause it is."

"No. It's not. We're trying to get ahead of these Hera and Zeus characters. We've got no idea who they are. All we know is what they want. Immortality. Director Cooper decided that the best course of action is to make sure that every single tall tale or legend about immortality be safeguarded from these immortality chasers."

"Wait." Klaus shook his head. "You really think that someone will walk into Christmas Town and steal this gold wreath *during* the holiday season? The Holy Grail legend isn't even *true*."

T-Bone nodded. "Be that as it may, Director Cooper wants to be safe. Besides, the holiday season would be the best time to abscond with the wreath. The town gets flooded with visitors and workers who visit Christmas Town, thinking it's nothing more than a gimmicky tourist destination. It would be the best time to sneak in and blend in with the higher number of unfamiliar faces." He pauses, taking the time to sit back into his chair, crossing his arms and giving me one hell of a stare-down. "Good thing it's your hometown. You'll have an advantage."

And just like that, I have to go back home for the first time since I was eighteen years old.

Fuck.

## 3

## RAYA

*Sweet echoing blood bag.*

There he is.

*Agent Klaus Thorsen.*

No other agent in FUC has a reputation quite like him. In fact, Agent Thorsen is kind of legendary. He always refuses to work with a partner. He stomps around in his motorcycle boots like he owns the place. He's a good agent with exceptional statistics, even though he barely speaks to anyone other than Director Cooper.

I hate him.

Not because he's a bad guy or even because he's a good one, albeit unconventional.

Nope. I don't like Klaus Thorsen because he's too hot. Men who are *that* good-looking always know it down to their bone—if you know what I mean. They believe they're a gift to every other human.

From what I've seen of Klaus around the Academy, he's like that. He pretends he doesn't see people fawning over him with his shoulder-length ash-blond hair and his brooding green eyes.

Real talk? The man bun is a *ridiculous* trend.

On Klaus Thorsen? It's not a man bun.

It's a fucking halo. It's a damn crown of sexiness.

Not that I would *ever* admit this out loud to *anyone*.

I'll have to put my lust on serious lockdown and make sure Klaus knows just how much I hate his dumb, sexy, handsome, moody face.

I'm on a mission, yes, but not only for FUC. I'm here to make a name for myself, and I can't do that if Klaus Sex God distracts me every time he flips his hair like a teenage cheerleader.

Maybe I'll attack him with a pair of scissors as soon as he falls asleep. There's a good chance he draws all of his power from his hair like good ol' Samson.

I drop my duffel beside his and give him a cursory head nod. I don't blush—*much*.

"You're the noob they paired me with?" His voice is a deep baritone that rumbles out of him like a motorcycle revving first thing in the morning.

*Oh, my flight.*

He's so good-looking I *almost* miss the aggression in his tone.

Almost.

His green eyes are narrowed toward me as he takes in my not-so-winter gear. My trusty and favorite leather jacket might not be the warmest or thickest protection against the northern wind, but it's sort of my armor.

I refuse to ride into battle without it and my combat boots.

Klaus spends too long of a second on my legs for his perusal to be professional. Perhaps that's all in my head. I roll my shoulders back and give him my best annoyed glare.

"I'm Agent Slaski." I don't hold out my hand for a shake.

No chance in hell am I allowing any contact between us. I've got no clue how I'll react to that, and the very last thing I need is to blush because a cute guy touches me.

This isn't middle school, and I'm not some fawning little bat.

I'm a newly minted FUC agent and a grown woman in complete control of her libido. Who cares if his hair smells like pine trees and sandalwood? I certainly don't notice that his eyes are the color of incandescent emeralds. Nor do I pay *any* attention to his ass when he turns around to grab his duffel bag off the ground.

Because if I *did* notice his butt, I'd have to write an ode to it.

*Good starry sky above.*

Who knew men's tushes could come in that shape? I sure didn't. His ass and his hair are locked in a competition for which body part attracts more of my attention.

Right now, it's a tied score.

"I don't care who you are, agent. All I care about is getting the job done as quickly as humanly possible. I don't want to fuck this up. Got it?"

I arch a brow at him and cock my hip. "Are you serious right now?"

"What?"

"Did you really tell a fellow agent not to fuck up a mission? Do you really think it's necessary to warn me that we have a job to do?"

"Sure feels like the newer generations of agents are too soft. Besides, I don't think a first-timer is an agent. *Way* too green."

I grin at him, flashing my incisors. I've never bitten a human, but he's a second away from making me change my mind.

*Oh, buddy. Poor, sweet, innocent little reindeer. Welcome to my trap, jerkface.*

"Yeah?" My smirk turns saccharine. "You don't find the newer agents equipped to cope with the field?"

Klaus shrugs. "Nope."

"Is that so, Agent Thorsen?" Director Alyce Cooper snaps, coming up behind him.

His jaw clenches, and he shoots me a murderous and accusatory glance. His gaze screams for revenge.

*You can try, pretty boy.*

And, by Bela Lugosi's fangs, the man sure is a tasty dish.

Klaus flashes his own teeth at me in a threatening promise before facing our boss. "Sorry, Director."

"No, you're not," she shoots back. "Don't try to backtrack now, Klaus. I heard you loud and clear. Maybe if you've got so many opinions about the quality of the agents coming through the program, I should add you to the next roster of teachers."

Klaus blanches visibly, and Director Cooper, the sly lady she is, relishes his momentary panic.

"I think I'll do that," she goes on. "We'll see how things go with this one." She juts her chin toward me. "You ready, Agent Slaski 2.0?"

I try to stifle my reaction to her words, but I'm pretty sure Klaus notices my back stiffening. Agent Slaski 2.0? Is that really how my boss sees me?

Not going to lie. That hurts.

I spent all my school years being told just how awesome my sister is. I don't need it for the rest of my career. Why couldn't Vera stay a lawyer? Damn her and her perfection.

Every time I walked into a new class in high school, the teacher would take one look at my last name and *expect* me to perform at the same level as Vera. Was it my fault I didn't enjoy studying or staying still as much as her? No. It didn't stop *everyone* from comparing us—and for finding me seriously *lacking*.

For once in my life, I would love to be noticed and praised for my own achievement. For being Raya Slaski. For simply being little old me with my nose ring, tattoos, leather jacket addiction, and badass attitude.

"Are you ready to go?" Director Cooper asks me.

"I am, yes."

"Good. I wanted to come and personally see you off. This wreath you have to protect? It's an important artifact. Whether it is the Holy Grail melted down into a wreath or not is irrelevant. Hell, the fact that it isn't actually magical isn't even significant. What matters is that all of Christmas Town depends on the wreath to propagate their economy because people come from far and wide to see the supposedly-magical wreath. Not to mention putting a stop to Vitality Holdings and uncovering the identities of Hera and Zeus. A lot is riding on this."

"Yes, ma'am. Of course." I give her my best and most reassuring nod. My legs don't shake, nor do I feel the weight of my entire future career looming overhead.

"I'll keep the mission on course," Klaus cuts in, throwing his duffel over his shoulder.

"Make sure that you do, or else I'll be sending you to the *northiest* north to ever north every holiday season. You can kiss your beach Christmases goodbye if you fuck this up."

Klaus's eyes cut to mine. "Sure thing, Director."

"I haven't forgotten your last slip-up, Klaus. I might remand you to a classroom yet." With another long and heavy scrutiny of us, Director Cooper turns on her heels and leaves the hangar.

I watch her leave, taken in by the sheer magnitude her

presence commands. She is one impressive woman. I totally want to be her when I grow up.

---

THE FLIGHT FROM FUCN'A, all the way to Christmas Town, is long and quite possibly the most turbulent flight I've ever been on.

I've gone skydiving, so that's saying something.

The airplane isn't exactly big, but it's large enough that Klaus is sitting a few feet away from me. If I didn't know any better, I would assume the big muscle-man is *scared* of flying. I swear, his jaw looks *that* much more clenched.

I could've *sworn* I saw him watching breathing exercises on his tablet during takeoff.

Not that there is anything wrong with that.

It's nice to see that the Klaus *I-only-ever-scowl* Thorsen has a weak spot. It makes him a little more human and a little less *scary-agent-with-more-experience*.

Klaus hasn't spoken a word to me since his warning earlier. I'm so bored part of me wants to poke at his patience. I curb the impulse. The last thing we need on this mission is more animosity.

This has to go perfectly well. I *have* to prove myself a good agent in my own right. Not because I have the Slaski last name but because of my own actions.

I will *not* be Agent Slaski 2.0.

I am Raya, my very own bat. Hear me echolocate!

If Man-Bun Klaus gets in my way?

Well, he'll be playing a whole different kind of reindeer game.

I flip open the file T-Bone gave me and read over the case for the millionth time. It seems pretty straightforward.

Go to Christmas Town, guard the gold wreath, and ensure no one gets their hands on it.

It's basically a security guard job.

Or it would be. These Hera and Zeus characters seem to have a whole lot of cash at their disposal. We have to be very careful. They somehow managed to infiltrate and blackmail an agent in the Cryptozoian Council. Klaus and I will have to be aware of our surroundings at all times. For all we know, there is already a mole in Santa's workshop, vying for the wreath.

"Do you think we should interview people as soon as we land?" I ask after a bout of turbulence so bad I'd half-thought we would fall out of the sky. "Way I see it we should ingratiate ourselves to Santa and his staff. Probably the local police force, too. The more we know, the better we can spot a mole if there is one."

Despite his pallor, Klaus rolls his eyes and doesn't look up from his tablet. I don't know what he's doing on there, but it seems to have all of his attention, the big—beautiful—ass.

"Klaus, seriously. I would appreciate a moment of your time to discuss strategy." *Especially since there's nothing else to do and it's doing my head in.*

"There's no strategy to discuss," he snaps, still not looking away from his device. "We land. We guard. Christmas ends. Back to the Academy. Final."

I purse my lips at him in serious displeasure. Of course, I *knew* his reputation before we even got onto the plane, but this surliness is next level.

"If someone pissed in your tinsel, it sure wasn't me. We need to be a team on this. A little commun—"

"Do. Not. Make. Christmas. Jokes." He enunciates every word and every syllable like a threat.

Or what would be a threat if he were talking to anyone else. But he's talking to me. I can out-stubborn the reindeer any day.

"You don't like Christmas?" I add a twinge of humor to my tone. Not quite teasing but not quite understanding. It's made to antagonize, and why not? I can give as good as I get. I've got a whole life of practice.

The man is a reindeer shifter who abhors Christmas. Fascinating, really. Freud and his buddies would have a collective *brain-gasm* if they got to work with him.

Right then and there, I nickname him Blitzen. It sounds sexy but grumpy, very much like the dude himself.

Klaus doesn't answer, but judging by the firm set of his jaw, he is trying *very* hard not to say anything.

*Point to me.*

So much for being a team.

4

**KLAUS**

*Sweet suffering Rudolph.*

Raya Slaski is one annoying—temptingly hot—woman.

It's not her fault that *everything* she does is downright aggravating. Not to mention gratingly sexy.

I should probably try to work with her. Be a team. I sure don't want Director Cooper to make good on her threat and actually put me on the teaching roster. I'd make a horrible teacher. I don't have the patience for it.

Case in point: I don't have the composure to sit so close to Raya on this bumpy-ass flight.

What's this plane made of anyway? Weld-together toy cars? I swear to the good lords of flight, I can *feel* every gust of wind. If we don't land soon, I will pass out and make a total idiot of myself.

Not that it'll take much.

Anytime I look in Raya's direction too long, I get a little bit dizzy. The silver hoop through her right nostril blinks at me every time I glance up. I want to flick it with my finger and trace the delicate line of Raya's nose all the way to that forehead of hers. A vein pops out of it every time I say something she disagrees with, so basically every time I open my mouth.

It's hilarious.

It's also a little hot.

Raya has a hard time containing her emotions, which means that she has every chance of being one hell of a firecracker in bed. I shake my head to loosen the thought. Getting all turned around because my so-called partner has pretty eyes, lush chocolate-brown waves, and a full red mouth won't help my career.

"We'll be landing soon," the pilot indicates with a loud shout over the plane's unnaturally loud din.

Seriously. Soldered tin roofs with wings does not an airplane make.

I give the woman a thankful nod and slide my tablet into my duffel. The flight is turbulent as hell, but at least, it's coming to an end. The rest of the trek to Christmas Town has to be done by sleigh.

Yup.

*Sleigh.*

Because going to Christmas Town isn't ridiculous enough, our only possible mode of transportation is a sleigh. I don't know if Raya has been briefed about that part yet, but she's spent the entire flight reading the case file.

*Like that will help you where we're heading.*

Christmas Town is the fakest, most duplicitous place on earth.

Raya will need a lot more than studying the case notes to survive out here for two weeks. She's going to learn the truth about a lot of things. Like how hot chocolate can easily be doctored with a fair amount of salt. How garlands can be used as rope. How ornaments can be used as missiles.

It's not all tinsel and carols.

It's taunting and contempt.

The landing, done on a very narrow strip of land at the very tip of Canada, is horrible. We lurch to the left, to the right, tip forward. Probably do a fairly good impression of the twist.

By the time the front wheels collide with the permafrost ground, I'm greener than a fir tree.

*Shit.*

I'm not even in town yet, and I'm already dropping Christmas metaphors.

I shake my head and scrub my scalp with my fingers to dislodge any other latent Christmas vocabulary that wants to make its way out. Better I do it in my thoughts than out loud for Raya to hear.

Her pale face is ashen, her knuckles white as she clutches the armrests. I feel bad for her. This is hardly a fun flight, and as someone who hates flying in general, that's saying something.

"It's normal for it to be like this out here." The words leave my mouth before I can think better of it.

Raya looks up and meets my gaze with a grateful nod. It knocks out the tiny gulp of air still holding firm in my lungs. I really need to remember that this trip is about one thing and one thing only.

Securing solo missions for the next little while—and ensuring I don't end up in the classroom.

I can't get preoccupied with my history, no matter how much my family and the town will try to rope me into their drama. *Again.*

And I most definitely *cannot* be distracted by the batty lady with sparkling eyes, cheeky mouth, and no-bullshit attitude.

She, with her nose ring and cranberry lips, needs to stay

the hell away from me.

Once we've landed, the pilot leaves the small cabin with a smile. "We made it." Her surprise is shocking, but I try not to let it get to me. "Storm is rolling in, so you better be quick about it."

"Thanks," I grumble.

Raya rolls her shoulders back, and she tries to be tough, but the vein on her forehead is trembling. Part of me wants to give her a hard time for being a chicken. The other part of me wants to wrap her up in my arms and reassure her that it'll be all right.

I've got no clue where that comes from, but I beat it back like a kid who gets a lump of coal on Christmas morning.

*For fuck's sake. Enough with the Christmas stuff, Klaus. You're better than that.*

"Director Cooper told me you know how to get to the village from here?" The pilot forms it as a question, unsure what to do with the information.

I answer with a vague head nod, but of course, Raya hears the exchange and crosses her arms. "Sorry, are you telling me that you know where this mysterious Santa village is? And what? I'm just supposed to take your word for it that you can bring us there safely and in one piece?"

I keep my face an unreadable mask, but Raya isn't done. She goes on. "Seriously. How can you know where we're going? Do you get a map? I didn't. I'd like to examine it before we head out."

The pilot chuckles. "Do you have *any* idea who Klaus is?" she asks. I give her the most threatening death glare I can muster, but she misses it entirely. How many people know my secret? Alyce sure didn't uphold our whole secrecy deal. "Klaus here is *from* Christmas Town."

Raya's head snaps in my direction. Her big hazel eyes

nearly pop right out of her head with pure jubilation. "Is this for real?"

I don't respond.

"Oh, sweet echolocation. The big grumpy badass is actually from *Christmas Town*? You. A reindeer. From Christmas Town." She doesn't even try to contain her giggles. "Why doesn't everyone know about this?"

"Because it's my own personal business, and I don't like to talk about it."

"I don't know that you'll have much choice after this assignment, *Blitzen*."

My vision goes red at the sound of the nickname. "Do. Not. Call. Me. That."

"You know, you're pretty much the king of monosyllabic conversations. You speak in full sentences, technically speaking, but you punctuate each word with a pause. It's the strangest thing."

"It's not strange. It's by design. My link to Christmas Town is strictly on a need-to-know basis. You're sworn to secrecy."

"By who?" she shoots back, relishing this moment way too much. The vein in her forehead pretty much winks at me.

For one insane second, I almost lean over to shut her up with my mouth. I bet her lips taste like cranberries. They sure are red enough for it. I stuff my hands into my pockets to keep from reaching out to Raya and doing something we will both definitely fucking regret.

"You two are gonna have so much fun together," the pilot cackles on the way back into her so-called craft. "Happy tidings and all that good stuff."

Without sparing Raya another look, I lumber over to the small little hangar. The walls are made of sturdy concrete, but even they seem to shake and shimmy in the strong northern wind. Using the sleigh all the way to town is going to suck. It'll be cold and windy.

Raya will be sharing a very narrow seat with me. With any luck, there will be *two* blankets in the sleigh because I sure don't feel like sharing my close personal space with her.

Not now. Not ever.

I'll take my chances with hypothermia.

The sleigh is bright red with a black leather runner covered with a thick plaid blanket. The eight non-shifter reindeer huff and move their hooves through the thick snow as Raya and I pile our things at our feet. I know exactly how the animals and their sleigh got here, but I'm not offering Raya that information. If she has any questions, she can bug one of the locals when we arrive. I'm not going to explain anything or interact with the town any more than I need to.

"Family of yours?" She juts her chin toward the reindeer.

*Of course, that's what she asks.* That mouth of her is quirked up in a sly smirk, and I don't know if I want to dish the diss right back or kiss her quiet.

Probably shouldn't do either of those.

Instead, I choose to ignore her.

Raya rolls her eyes, clicking her tongue. "You're gonna need some kind of sense of humor if you're going to be a reindeer shifter in Christmas Town this time of year."

It's on the *tip* of my tongue to tell her that I'm all too familiar with the village, but I don't. It would only invite more questions, and I'm not feeling chatty at all. It's colder than a snowman's ball sac. I forgot how damn freezing it gets here during the holidays.

Only *one* of the reasons I left and never returned.

*Please, do* not *let Mom and Dad know I'm on my way.*

That's the very last thing I need. I don't want Nosy Raya

to know anything about me, my family, or the reasons why I left them behind the second I was old enough to head out on my own.

Really, when you tell people you *hate* Christmas, they look at you like you've got horns. Not the antlers of a reindeer. No. Some real satanic ones.

No one *wants* to believe that someone can actually hate a holiday that is all about love, joy, and giving.

These people seem to forget that it's actually not the season of giving but the season of *lies*.

Seriously.

It's the time of year where everyone pretends to like each other just long enough to overeat and overdrink after overspending.

My best Christmas memories are all on a beach somewhere, drunk off my ass. The hotter, the more secluded, the better. If that makes me hateful, then so be it. My family sure thinks it makes me villainous to hate Christmas.

"Are you going to tell me how a reindeer from Christmas Town ended up as a FUC agent?"

"No."

Raya chuckles softly. "How long is the ride into town?"

"Long."

"Right. How long? Long enough for me to needle all of the information I want out of you?"

I ignore her and climb onto the sleigh. The sound of her laughter is soft and musical. Hell, it's almost *pleasing*. I shake the thought right out of my head and focus on checking the reins.

"Your name is Klaus, and you lived in Santa *Claus'* town. Is he your godfather? Are you named for him? You've gotta gimme something. I'm dying to know how any of this happened."

"No."

"Oh, come on. We're partners."

"We are *not* partners, and unless you're willing to lay down all of your family's reactions to the Bloody Doctor, I suggest you drop the whole twenty-questions act."

Raya arches a brow at me, unfazed. "You think I won't talk about my aunt for hours? I will. I studied the hell out of her crimes. The way I see it, the more I know about monsters like her, the more equipped I am to deal with them. Family or not, evil is evil."

"Agreed," I grumble back with no further explanation.

That shuts Raya up, but I can see the wheels in her head spinning with her next question.

This is going to be the longest two weeks of my life.

5
_______

## RAYA

*Dear candy cane gods.*

This is next-level intense.

When I first learned that I would be posted in Christmas Town *during* Christmas, I expected the whole village to be holiday-crazed. How could it be anything else than every Yule-time cliché imaginable?

I anticipated decorations and lights everywhere. Cheery people rushing busily in the streets on the way to the workshops. Maybe even some super fragrant treats scenting the cold, crisp winter air.

In truth, nothing—and I mean absolutely *nothing*—could have prepared me for this.

The big red, green, gold, and silver sign that announces our arrival in town is strung up with lights. They twinkle and shimmy a greeting for us as we pass by. I hold my breath, but I'm not sure why. It's not excitement, exactly. It's not nerves, either.

It's a whole new kind of emotion I can't name. It feels a little bit sacred, like a long-lost part of me is coming back to life.

So fucking weird.

My tummy is full of little explosions that travel up my chest and sit at the base of my throat. If I don't keep my mouth shut, I'm liable to *ooh* and *aah* like a little kid.

Real talk?

I stopped believing in Santa Claus a *very* long time ago. To be riding into his village like it's nothing? That's a little dizzying. I'm half expecting Director Cooper to pop out with a camera, laughing at me for falling for this fake mission.

Then she would kick me out because I'm not as good as my sister.

"You okay?" Klaus asks, giving me a rare—but sexy—worried frown.

"Fine," I respond, trying to bat away the bad and invasive thoughts.

He rolls his eyes, his concern replaced with annoyance. "Don't let any of this faze you. This place isn't all that it's cracked up to be."

I snort. "Who *hurt* you?" I'm trying to be funny, but Klaus' head snaps up, and his features darken. He doesn't find me hilarious. At all. "Touchy," I mumble.

Klaus ignores me and leads the sleigh through the small town. The main street is wide enough to accommodate three or four sleighs. It's lined with shops and businesses that knock at my curiosity with all the chill of a melting snowman.

Every storefront is decked out with lights and tinsel, with garlands and ornaments. It's basically a Christmas feast for all five senses.

Part of me wants to get directly to work, while another wants to jump down from the sleigh and explore this incredible little town.

I challenge *anyone* to be in this magical place and not go full *kid.*

Impossible.

At least, unless your name is Klaus Thorsen and you're basically made of steel. He glares at every person we pass, sending daggers toward most stores.

I don't know what the man has against his hometown, but he really needs to cool his eggnog or heat up his chestnuts.

I open my mouth to share my hilarious Christmas jokes, but his deep-set frown has me curbing my mischievous jabs.

If we're working together as a team, maybe I shouldn't antagonize him simply because it's fun to rile him up. I roll my shoulders back and ignore him, focusing instead on my pleasant surroundings.

It's hard to imagine how someone would infiltrate this place, but if I've learned anything from the world during my time with FUC and the Academy, it's that everyone has a price.

It doesn't matter if it's money or favors or even *things.*

Everyone can be lured into a bad situation.

"We're here," Klaus announces, pulling up in front of a massive bed and breakfast.

It's something out of a fairytale. The log building is covered in snow, looking more like a giant gingerbread house than an inn. There are red and green ornaments shimmering from every cornice and twinkling lights framing every window and door. It casts happy little illuminated dances against the pure white snow.

The Jingle Bell Inn is adorable, but the owners obviously take great pride in every aspect of their business. I hop down from the sleigh, eager to see the inside of the building. It takes me only a moment to swing my duffel over my shoulder. Klaus mutters something to me, but I don't hear him. I'm way too busy scampering up the steps.

Am I a fully grown woman with a penchant for leather and motorcycles getting excited about Christmas? Yes. So what? There are no rules out there stating that I need to be a grouch because I'm an adult.

Klaus can be grinch enough for both of us.

The second the door swings open, a fragrant wall of gingerbread spice and mint hit me. It's warm and comforting. I've got an urge to curl up the huge fireplace to read. Me! The lady who has a hard time sitting still for more than a minute at a time.

This place really does have magical powers.

My guess is that nostalgia is the kicker. It clenches your heart and memories tight until you can't help but give in to the spirit of things.

The short woman behind the enormous log desk waves me forward. Her white hair spills out of her crisp and starched lace bonnet. It matches the apron draped over her bright red dress, patterned over with poinsettias and holly.

"Hello, there." Her voice is warm and welcoming, like a cup of hot cocoa. "How were your travels into town?"

"Fine, thanks. I'm wondering if my room is ready. Reservations under Raya Slaski." As I drop my heavy bag onto the floor, continuing my visual feast of the inn, the woman flips through a big leather-bound book. The thick cream paper makes a loud *whoosh* noise every time she turns the pages. It almost keeps time to the Christmas song wafting from a small record player sitting in a place of honor beside a huge Christmas tree. "Maybe it's under Kl—"

"The reservations are made under your name," Klaus snaps, letting the door slam behind him. "Raya Slaski. Two rooms."

"Oh, yes," the cheery lady chortles. "There you are. First time in town?" She narrows her gaze as she tries to stare directly into Klaus's eye, but he purposefully avoids her.

The jerk.

Doesn't he want to tell this nice person that he's from here? Probably not. He doesn't seem to be too pleased with being back home again.

"I'm Mrs. Jingle. Let me know if you need anything." She slides two thick candy cane keychains onto the desk, each holding a heavy skeleton key made of shiny metal that looks way too much like gold.

"Thanks so much," I gush. The second I'm in my room I'm guzzling hot cocoa like it's going out of style.

"Breakfast is served from six until ten. Lunch is at noon and runs through to one most days. The first dinner set is at six, but there is a late sitting at nine if that's better." She beams at me, and I return the sentiment. "You don't want to miss my waffle tree in the morning."

"Waffle tree?" I ask, my mouth already watering.

"Every morning during the holidays, I make a big stack of waffles in the shape of a Christmas tree. All the fixings you could want decorate it. It's almost too pretty to eat."

"That sounds amazing. I can't wait."

"No, thanks," Klaus grumbles as he grabs his key and disappears down the hall.

I shoot our host an apologetic smile and race after him. "Hey, you might want to ease on the attitude if you want this mission to be successful. In case you've forgotten, we need the townspeople's cooperation for this to work."

Klaus spins on his heels, nearly crashing into me. He has to reach out and steady me before I land flat on my ass. "Don't tell me how to do my job, noob. I know what needs to happen."

"Well, if you don't want them to know who you are, maybe behaving in a completely different way than your usual sunny self would be to your benefit."

His eyes turn cold, but he doesn't respond, choosing instead to let me go. I stumble back but quickly find my balance. He takes the steps two at a time, away from me and toward his room.

If I had the time, I would take a look around and maybe snap a few pictures to show my parents. That's not my main concern right now. Instead, I chase after Klaus, hissing his name under my breath as to not bother the other guests.

He unlocks his door and tries to slam it in my face, but thankfully, I manage to shove my heavy boot to stop its progress. Klaus glares at me. "What are you doing?"

"Well, before you retreat into your room and go full recluse, we need to discuss our strategy. This is why we should have talked about it in the plane or in the sleigh."

"We can discuss it in the morning. I need a nap and some food."

I scowl, sensing the lie. He's got every intention of going off on his own as soon as he gets rid of me. "Do you *not* remember Director Cooper's warning? If you fuck this up, it'll be the classroom for you. We need to work together." I arch a brow at him with my arms crossed, waiting for his response.

Klaus's eyes burn into mine. The dude is *pissed*. "I told you. I work better alone. Now, leave me be. I need a nap," he says through gritted teeth.

Really, his anger shouldn't be an aphrodisiac. I *know* I should click my tongue at him and ignore his little *mantrum*, but his annoyance is kind of *way* delicious. I swear, the more furious Klaus is, the sexier he becomes.

That's saying something.

The man already has a lot going for him. Between his long hair, beard, and thousands of tattoos, he's already dangerous to my sanity. Make him frown at me with that glare? I want to push *all* of his buttons.

That's why it takes all of my self-control not to tell him that I'll be going off without him. If he wants to dick around, that's on him.

I don't need Klaus to do my job.

## 6

# KLAUS

*A whole bag of stinking bah, humbug!*

The décor of the bed and breakfast is a little much for me.

It's overwhelming outside, but that's nothing to the suffocating avalanche of so-called Christmas cheer in my room. The thick bright red carpet is offset by blinding white walls with enough shimmer in them to give me a headache.

I know for a *fact* that the paint shade is called Freshly Fallen Snow. It definitely lives up to its namesake.

The comforter is a thick green blanket that would be great camouflage in a fir forest. The pillows are all kinds of Christmas themes and colors, while the scent of sugar cookies seems to be pumped through the vents every two minutes.

My stomach rolls from its overwhelming aroma.

I need to get the hell out of here.

I'm claustrophobic and in severe danger of going into over-Christmas shock.

It's like septic shock, only instead of slow, agonizing

death, it's a... well, slow and agonizing death without the death part.

With a mumbled string of curses at being back in my hometown, I slide my boots back on and grab my jacket. Walking through town will hardly give me any kind of reprieve, but at least it won't feel like the walls are closing in to strangle me with Christmas cheer.

I. Hate. The. Holidays.

Mrs. Jingle gives me a warm smile from behind the counter as I head out the door. She waves and giggles like an elf putting clothes on a naked doll. "Have a fun walk-around, dear."

I think I grumble something back to her, but I don't know what. I definitely don't want to interact with her too much for fear she'll recognize me.

I need fresh air and distance from all of this stuff that reminds me of my childhood.

As soon as the wintry blast of wind hits my face, pelting me with crisp and almost painful wind, I close my eyes. I let the cold seep into my skin to temper my nerves. After a few deep gulps, I turn toward the center of town. If I'm going to be stuck here, I might as well take a spin around the village core to get my bearings and see what's changed since I was here last.

The hot chocolate shop is still opened right beside the bakery. Every third business is a specialty ornament store, from precious materials to more affordable ones. There are clothing stores, but everything is patterned over with holiday *stuff*. The shopkeepers and the townsfolk rush around like busy little elves they are, bustling from one store to the other.

They're not *actually* elves. That's simply what people

from Christmas Town call themselves, just like people from Ontario are Ontarians.

I have a better name for these people than *elves*, but I digress.

What I *really* want to do is grab the first person I see and shake them out of their Christmas stupor.

It won't help.

Christmas Town is literally the most Christmasy place in the world. It makes Whoville look like the Grinch's cave.

It's *that* bad.

I scan the main street, trying to decide who I should interview first.

Back in the day, I would have started with the bakery or the hot chocolate shop. The married couple that owns those two businesses were always up on the current gossip.

That's precisely why I can't start with them. The second Carol and Evergreen Trimmings learn that I'm back in town, the sooner my parents will track me down and force me to join them for dinner.

*No. Fucking. Thanks.*

I flip the collar of my coat up to shield my face. As if the long hair and beard didn't hide my identity from the people who used to know me. They're unlikely to recognize me. I was eighteen the last time I was here.

I never intended to return, but now that I'm here, I have to do my job as efficiently and quickly as possible. If all this is put to rest before the twenty-fifth, I might actually be able to celebrate Christmas on a warm, sandy beach with a bikini-clad stranger who redefines the naughty list.

"Well, well, well." Raya grins as she walks up to me. A large red and white bag dangles from her left hand while the other is wrapped around a huge cup of hot chocolate. "If

I didn't know any better, I'd say that Grumpy Blitzen is out for a walk around his hometown."

A low growl vibrates at the back of my throat. "Don't call me that."

It's a wonder of life that she's picked that name out of all of the possibilities. It's like a part of her *knows* about my past.

Impossible.

Raya's brows disappear under her brand-new bright red tuque with a silver and white pompom. It jiggles as she laughs. "Oh, come on. Don't be such a grinch. This place is actually really cool. I can't get over how beautiful everything is. Every shop is super committed to the theme, and I appreciate the hell out of it. Or..." She giggles. "I appreciate the *tinsel* out of it." She continues to chuckle softly as she takes a sip of her drink. Her eyes roll back, and she moans. "This is legit the *best* thing I've ever had in my mouth. The hot chocolate is hot but not so much so that it burns my mouth. And the smoothness? It's like swallowing silky chocolate before it does a happy dance in my belly."

I don't know why her description of her beverage sounds so sensual, but it is. I swallow hard and resist the urge to dunk my head in one of the snowbanks lining the street to cool myself down.

"I'm out exploring. Doing recon at the same time. Is that what you're doing too? Or are you on your way to your family's place?"

"I needed out of my room."

"It's really stunning out here. I'm wondering where to go for dinner. Literally every place looks like it'll be amazing. Tell me where to eat."

"No."

"Then join me."

"No," I repeat.

"*Klaus?*"

My breath catches, but I don't have to turn around to know who has spoken my name. Raya's eyes grow to the size of massive ornaments, and a smirk plays across those delectable red lips of hers.

"Hey, Dad," I mumble before the man engulfs me in a hug that smells like pine and sugar cookies. It's the smell of home, but it's also the scent of my own personal hell.

I pull away from him and will Raya away. She stands there, looking on with a dopey grin on her ridiculously lovely face.

"And who might you be? Did my son finally bring a lady home to meet the family?"

Raya bursts out laughing. "No. Oh, no. We're here on assignment."

Dad's shoulders deflate. "Well, then you must be his partner." He holds out his hand for Raya to shake. "Welcome to our little slice of paradise."

She beams at him. "It really is something else."

"You two need to come over for dinner," Dad gushes like it's the idea of the century.

Raya glances at me, and I do everything in my power to silently plead with her to refuse.

She doesn't.

"I'd love to," she answers. "If this grinchy grinch-grinch won't come along, it's his loss."

"Absolutely," Dad agrees, but I can see the hope brimming out of his eyes. "Whaddya say, son? Come for dinner."

"Fine," I grumble.

What else can I do? I get my stubborn streak from my father. If I don't agree, he's going to start telling Raya all kinds of embarrassing stories until I fold.

My childhood home is a small two-story log structure in one of the neighborhoods off the main drag. The decorations *never* come down. My parents keep the place decked out all year round, and none of their neighbors complain— because they do the same.

It's always *almost* Christmas when you live in Christmas Town.

No sooner is Santa back in his leather armchair with a spiked hot chocolate than the countdown for the next year begins.

Dad points to a few ornaments hanging from the big lit-up Douglas tree that frames the front of the house. "Klaus made those when he was a little boy."

"I can see he was very talented." Raya's smile makes it pretty damn obvious that she's enjoying this quite a bit.

I open my mouth to unleash some kind of self-preserving quip, but the words die on my lips when the front door swings open. My mother, clad in a bright red dress and a deep green apron, clasps her hand under her trembling chin. Her blonde hair has started going gray, but it makes her look that much more dignified. She's aged quite a bit during my absence. My heart breaks a little bit, but I try to ignore the pain.

"Is that my boy?" she shouts, tearing down the stairs. She hugs me tight, saying all kinds of things that make me feel like the world's biggest jerk for not visiting at least a couple of times.

"Holly, this is Klaus's partner, Raya," Dad announces.

Mom drops me like a hot chestnut and rushes to Raya. She cups the newbie agent's face in her hands and gasps. "My tinsel, but you are beautiful. A shifter, too, no doubt?"

Raya nods. "Vampire bat."

Mom laughs. "Oh, isn't that interesting. Positively Halloweeny! Have no fear. We'll help you feel right at home." She drags Raya into the house and offers her a pair of thick knit slippers.

Raya slips them on and moves her feet around. "These are amazing. How do you get them so soft and thick?"

Mom taps her nose. "That's a secret. It's Christmas Town magic." She adds a wink before leading Raya into the living room.

Of course the Christmas tree is up and so decorated it's a little hard to look straight at it. It's full of lights and ornaments that shimmy by the twinkling bulbs. Even the large, soft, tan leather couch has been Yuled. A reindeer throw is draped over it, showcasing what the Thorsen family is known for in this part of the world.

Reindeer rearing and training.

I plop into the sofa and cross my arms, unsure what to do with my hands. I spoke to my parents two weeks ago when they called to beg me to come home for the holidays. Before that, it had been a few months.

Before that? Probably a year.

My parents aren't bad people. They're actually *good*. It's not their fault I hold a grudge like a mother fucker. If only they had taken my side all those years ago, our relationship wouldn't be so tense.

"So," Mom says, sitting beside me on the couch. She pats my knee and grins. "Tell me why you're in town. I thought you were going back to that beach resort."

"We're here on business, Mom. I don't have time to do much but work."

"Nonsense," Raya interjects. "If your family wants to see

more of you while you're here for *Christmas*, I can totally pick up the slack."

"Not a chance. You're a noob. I'm not trusting you alone with this very important mission."

"Oh-oh," Dad chuckles, handing Raya a glass of eggnog so strong it could probably peel paint off the walls. The man loves his spiced rum. "Do I sense some tension in the team?"

Raya giggles as she takes a gulp of the drink. "This is my very first mission away from the Academy. I'm newly badged. Apparently, that means I'm green."

"Green is one of the best colors in the world. It's right there along with red." Mom nudges her elbow into my side. "But we can't ask you to work more because of this one. If he's here, you should be too." She rubs her hands together like a kid about to tear into a mountain of gifts. "I'm sure the local authorities will be enough help for you two to come to some of our holiday traditions."

"I'd love that." Raya means it, too.

That's when it hits me.

Raya didn't choose this mission any more than I did. I don't like Christmas or being in my hometown, but there is every chance that my partner misses her family. Maybe she wanted to spend the holidays with the rest of the Slaski bats and whatever it is nocturnal creatures do at Christmas.

Probably drink hot blood while dancing around a dead tree or something.

"It's settled," Mom announces. "You'll have Christmas dinner here. Oh, and you can't miss the cookie exchange." She continues rattling off all of the things she wants us to do.

I barely pay attention. My focus is a little wonky.

For some weird reason, I can't stop staring at the twinkling light playing across Raya's features. She's glowing and beautiful. Two things I definitely shouldn't notice about my newbie partner.

Or anyone, for that matter.

We're here to work.

Not to celebrate the holidays.

Not to reminisce about the past.

Not to drool over cranberry lips.

## 7

## RAYA

My evening with Klaus and his parents was one of the most illuminating nights of my life.

Not because of the millions of Christmas lights.

Nope.

It had everything to do with how Klaus interacted with his super-sweet parents. I don't have to be a genius to see that though there is a lot of love there, there was a breach of trust at one point. Klaus's parents know what caused it, and they're trying very hard to fix it.

The problem is that Klaus is the most stubborn man alive.

Must be the antlers on his head that make his skull so thick.

For some reason, I am *always* on the receiving end of his ornery streak. On the walk back to the Jingle Bell Inn last night, I gave Klaus a brief glimpse of my strategy. He shot down all of my ideas. He barely let me get in a word before launching into his own plans.

Apparently, all of mine were crap and reeked of my inexperience. He particularly didn't like it when I reminded him that though I might be green to him, it's one of the best colors in the world.

When I repeated his mother's words, the glare he gave me could have reheated a frozen hot chocolate.

Before we each retreated to our bedrooms, we didn't agree on a course of action. Yet, I'm way ahead of him. He might think that I'm nothing but a wet-behind-the-ears whelp, but I'm a good agent. I know the protocols forward and backward. Not to mention my killer instincts.

Our first stop today *has* to be the big man himself.

Klaus disagrees. He thinks we need to go to the local authorities first. Though he isn't wrong, he isn't right. The CTPD might very well need to know we're on their side, but nothing happens in this town without Santa knowing about it. At least, that's what Holly said. Since she's lived here much longer than her son, I'm siding with her on this.

Somehow, I manage to get Klaus to join me at Santa's workshop.

Probably because I threatened to have every meal with his parents while I'm in town. He doesn't need to know I still fully plan on doing this. Holly and Patridge Thorsen are wonderful people.

Santa's workshop doesn't look like any factory I've ever seen before in my life. It's a palace of Christmas proportions. The double-wide doors swing open to let us into a massive entryway. A huge chandelier hangs from above. The glimmering crystal ornaments are candy canes, sleighs, gingerbread cookies, and all kinds of Christmasy things. It's so beautiful and blinding I almost miss the patterned floor. The big red, white, and green tiles make a mosaic that probably looks like a Christmas scene when you climb up and down the huge swirling staircase.

A tiny little woman wrapped in yards and yards of

sparkling crimson material prances toward us with a wide smile. The apples of her cheeks are red with joy—and maybe some morning eggnog.

"Do my eyes deceive me, or is that little Blitz Thorsen I see?"

*What the tinsel?*

Why does *she* get to call him Blitz?

I nudge his side, and he swats my hadn't away with an annoyed growl. "We're *so* talking about *that* later."

Klaus groans. "No. Not up for discussion. Hi, Vanilla."

She beams at him. "Oh, and he remembers me. Imagine that. I suppose you're here to talk to the Big Man about the wreath?" Vanilla takes a dramatic look around the entryway and leans in close to us. "Between you and me, Santa is *very* concerned about this whole thing. The wreath can't be stolen. It would ruin everything good and pure about Christmas Town."

Klaus shrugs. "I'm not gonna let anything happen to the town."

"*We*," I correct. "*We* won't let anything happen to the town."

Vanilla nods. "That makes me feel better. Why would we trust our whole world to the man who left over a decade ago and never came back?"

Klaus's entire body stiffens. He runs a hand back through his hair. That's his tell. He does that when he's angry. Or pissed. Or annoyed.

Huh.

Seems that the rainbow of emotions that make up Klaus are all firmly in the *negative* column. I have a hard time reconciling who he is as a person and where he comes from. I was only joking when I asked him, *who hurt you?* But now, more than ever, I know there is a story behind his long absence from home—and his permanently surly attitude.

It might not be my mission to get to the bottom of it, but I will. I am, after all, the better agent.

---

VANILLA, Santa's head elf, business manager, and accountant, leads us down one of the many halls and to an enormous golden elevator. The doors slide open to the tune of "Santa Claus is Coming to Town," and the song continues as we travel down for what seems like miles. When we arrive at our destination, I am speechless.

The room—if it can even be *called* a room—is so big all of Christmas Town could fit in here three times over.

Little cabooses come and go in perpetual motion on a small train track across the busy factory floor.

Elves rush around, singing and laughing, and all-around having a good time while preparing toys... *and electronics.*

No joke. There is a handful of elves toiling over a series of tablets. *Making* the devices as easily as if they were icing a gingerbread man. It's a little bit dizzying. I want to pause and soak it all up, but this is hardly the time to fangirl over Santa's workshop.

Vanilla waves us forward, but I get the distinct impression that Klaus knows exactly where we're going. After all, the man drove us here in a damn *sleigh* from memory.

The head elf whistles a few bars of "Jingle All the Way," and one of the cabooses stops right in front of us. We hop in, piling into the minuscule car. Klaus's shoulder brushes against mine. I try not to get all gooey from the heat radiating off of him. I *try* not to take a big whiff of him, but the man smells way too damn good for my sanity.

I focus on the elves and the passing factory floor to keep my thoughts away from my leg pressed into his. Who knew man-thighs could be so damn thick and so damn appealing?

"Here we are," Vanilla announces before leaping down from the caboose. She hops toward a set of gold doors taller than Klaus.

The precious metal is patterned over with a forest scene where a reindeer presents a wreath to a young man. I want to take a few moments to look at the artwork, but Vanilla pushes it open.

"Boss, you've got some visitors."

A tall man sporting a full mane of pure white hair and a long silver beard looks up from a stack of papers. His brown eyes narrow, his skin a shade darker than I would have expected from a man who spends all of his time in the north, away from the sun. I'm a nocturnal creature with a sun allergy, but that isn't even a concern up here. Not in the dead of winter.

"Is that Blitz I see?" Santa's voice booms cheerfully across his office.

*Okay. Seriously?*

Everyone can call him Blitz but me? We're going to have some words, Blitz and I.

Klaus stiffens beside me at the same name that's got me more shaken than a snow globe

"Hey, Nik."

*Nik. Nik?*

Did Klaus *really* call Santa Nik like it's no big deal?

The older man crosses his arms and leans back into his chair, grinning wide. "Never thought I'd see you back in town, Blitz."

Klaus shrugs. "It's my job to go where they need me."

Santa—Nik?—smirks, amused. "Oh? And does FUC

treat you well? I can't imagine you volunteered for this mission in your hometown. I thought you'd rather be dead than come back here."

"Can we not do this?" Klaus grumbles.

I elbow him. "Dude. That's *Santa*. Do you *want* to be on the naughty list?"

Santa bursts out laughing, his head thrown back and his big belly jiggling. It's literally the happiest sight I've ever seen. Not-so-deep in my psyche, little Raya is giggling and clapping, chanting *again, again*.

"And you must be the partner. Raya Slaski." He smiles at me, and I almost curtsy. Why? No idea. This moment feels important, though. Like I'm meeting royalty.

"Yes. Hi. Hello."

Santa grins, but before he can say anything more, Klaus takes a step forward. "We're here for the wreath. Why don't you just show it to us? We need to know how secure it is."

Santa chuckles. "All business? Sure. We can do that, Blitz." He turns on his heels and makes his way to the opposing wall.

Right there, in a simple glass case, lies a gold wreath. It's nothing special, really. I don't really understand what all the fuss is about. I've seen nicer pieces in museums. But that's not why the wreath is important.

Apparently, it has magical powers.

If the legend is true, this thing is the Holy Gail. How nutso bananas is that? Who would melt down a chalice to make a decoration that can only be used once a year?

"It's been right here for a long time," Santa explains. "I don't know why it's an interesting relic all of sudden. It's most definitely *not* the Holy Grail."

"Who started that rumor then?" I ask.

Santa frowns. "I've got no clue. I think it happened around the early 1900s. There was a revival in the chase for the Holy Grail, and for some reason, the chase led them here." He rubs his beard. "Titus something... that was the fellow's name. He was a shifter, of course. He came here looking to buy the wreath. Vanilla's grandmother warned him that it wasn't for sale. That the town needs it for its magic, but the man didn't get it."

"Didn't get what?"

Santa shakes his head. "That magic isn't real. The wreath doesn't have magic in the abracadabra sense. It has the kind of magic that comes from belief and tradition." He takes the gold object in his hands, turning it over, showing it to me from all angles before letting me take it. "If this were to get stolen? Nothing would happen, really. But the repercussions for what it means to the town? What it means to the holiday? *That* is the danger."

I take my time to inspect it, but I'm not sure what I'm even looking for. We could have a fake wreath made and let the baddies steal it, but I can't see Klaus liking that plan. I bite my tongue, knowing I need to do better.

"So there is no magic to this town?"

Santa shrugs before pointing to a map of the world behind his desk. "I basically run a massive factory. I deliver some toys, sure, but there's no magic to it."

"The world's most famous toymaker is nothing more than a tinkerer with a penchant for family tradition and nepotism," Klaus grumbles.

"Guilty." Santa grins. "If people want to believe in magic? Well, that's on them. The real magic, the kind that is transcendent above anything else, is *stories*."

"That's true," I concur, a bit sad that magic isn't real. I should've known, though. I'm a grown woman who can shift into a one-ounce bat. That's not magic, no matter how improbable it is. It's shifter science.

It makes as much sense to me as the myth of the Holy Grail.

"*Santa* is a name. It's a state of mind that is passed down from father to son. My son Niko will take over for me when I'm too old, and so on and so forth."

Klaus mumbles something under his breath. I'm not sure what he says, but it doesn't sound too good. Something about *assholes being in charge of Christmas.*

That can't be right.

Could Klaus' whole issue with Christmas have something to do with the Santa family?

I make a plan to bug him about it later. If he doesn't open up, I can always go hang out with his parents. They'll be more than happy to share with me.

I would *never* admit this, but I miss my family. Even my sister. I've never spent a Christmas without them. I didn't exactly *expect* to miss the competition, but I do. Or maybe I just miss her—full stop.

"I need to secure the wreath, Nik." Klaus uses his authoritarian voice, pulling me from my less-than-pleasant thoughts. "It can stay in your office, but I'll want cameras on it at all times."

"*We'll* also need a list of everyone who has access to your office," I cut in, putting all of the emphasis I can on the *we*. If Klaus is still trying to make me butt out, he's got another think coming. "You'll need to limit the access to this area if you choose to keep the wreath here."

"I like this pairing." Santa's smirk is as mischievous as can be.

In the end, keeping the wreath where it's always been is the better course of action. If someone is in town to steal it or has been tapped by Vitality Holdings' puppet masters, Hera and Zeus, to steal it, they might make a move before we're ready if they know we're thinking about it changing things around. It would also put others in danger.

Santa leaves us in his office, apparently to go do some rounds of the workshop, but I have a feeling he left for Klaus' benefit.

"You know, I read up on reindeer before we left the Academy. I learned that they are very social animals who like to be in big herds. You're basically breaking your own instincts by being a lone reindeer. That tells me there's a story there."

"No," he grunts.

I laugh. "That's another thing I learned. Apparently, reindeer are *very* communicative and use all kinds of sounds to chat with their peers. You've got the grunts and grumbles down, my friend."

"I thought bats couldn't speak. Shouldn't you be super quiet? Only use echolocation or something?"

"Ha!" I nudge him with my elbow, mindful of the security camera I'm holding. "You did bat research. I'm choosing to see that as you reaching out to make a human connection."

He rolls his eyes and fiddles with a second camera.

All told, we are installing six tiny surveillance cameras that we will be able to access remotely from our phones and from a tiny little office in the depths of the workshop.

Are we *maybe* using the non-magical wreath as bait to catch Vitality Holdings' newest puppet? Yes. Absolutely.

"Are you gonna tell me why I can't call you Blitz?" I watch his reaction.

He flinches. "No."

"So there'll be another *no* when I ask why people here call you that?" I wait for ten Christmases to go by. Nothing. "Fine. Are you at least going to tell me why you don't like it here?" I ask, knowing he won't answer.

Klaus clenches his jaw down tight. "No."

"Why not? It would help me understand you better."

"And why do you need to understand me better?"

"We're partners."

"Only for a little while. Once this is all over, I'm not gonna have a partner for a long time. Best we keep things professional."

I click my tongue. "Being civil and holding a decent conversation with your partner *is* professional. Now, get your burly self up that ladder."

Klaus blanches. I don't imagine it, either. Under his beard, his entire face goes shades paler. I flashback to his boorish attitude on the plane, the breathing exercises he was doing on his tablet.

*Klaus is afraid of heights.*

"I'll do it." I start climbing up the ladder and hold out my hand for the camera and the bracket I'll need to screw to the wall.

"Don't gimme shit," he rumbles.

I scrunch up my face. "What? Why would I give you a hard time about being afraid of heights?"

"I'm not afraid," he snaps. His shoulders immediately deflate, and he runs a hand through his long luscious hair. "Sorry. I'm just..."

"Used to people giving you a hard time for it?"

He nods, avoiding my gaze.

"My big sister has a pretty big aversion to blood," I state. It's much easier to have this conversation with my back to him, focused on the screwdriver and nail. "As a vampire bat, that's not great. I always sort of teased her about it." I shrug. "It's not like there's anything wrong with her. We've all got our thing."

He snorts. "Yeah? And what's your thing?"

I turn and give him a saccharine smile. "Easy now, Blitz. That's *way* too personal." I add a wink because I'm feeling saucy.

What I *don't* anticipate is the heady look in Klaus's eyes. *That* almost makes me fall off the ladder and right into his big, strong, surly arms.

## 8

## KLAUS

Yesterday, while installing the cameras in Santa's office, Raya figured out my biggest fear. She was *this* close to also learning why I hate my hometown so much.

That irks her enough already.

If I told her I also hated Santa? She might have a coronary or something.

I've mostly been able to keep her questions about my childhood at bay. Not easy. She is one curious lady. You'd think that as a nocturnal creature she would be all grumpy, being up and about during the day.

Not a chance.

There is so very little sun here, in Christmas Town. Raya doesn't ever have to cover her face to keep the harmful rays away from her skin. Of course, it helps that it's colder than a snowman's asshole. Stubborn as she is, Raya still insists on wearing her leather jacket instead of the thick parka the Academy provided for her.

I would give her shit for it if she didn't look so damn *hot* in the stupidly uninsulated garment.

There is no way in hell that I *should* be attracted to the woman.

She's as infuriating as she is kind. Those two things don't really go together.

Raya didn't really *push* to learn the reasons why I don't like Christmas Town or heights. Oh, sure. She asks about it enough to make me want to kiss her quiet.

*We're going to ignore that I just said I want to kiss Raya and move right along.*

We've turned a small room in the bowels of the workshop into our own little security office. It's the first time in history that a security system has to be implemented, which is worrisome.

All morning, Vanilla has brought elves for us to interview. We don't really know what we're looking for. All we have to go on is what the Cryptozoian Council agent, Val Downer, shared. FUC uncovered that she was a mole a few months ago. The shadowy leaders of Vitality Holdings, calling themselves Hera and Zeus, injected a toxin into her bloodstream. If she didn't cooperate daily, they wouldn't send her the serum she needed to stay alive. They were literally blackmailing her with *death*.

It is difficult to interview the hundreds of people who make Christmas Town a possibility. We need to discover if anyone has fallen prey to the same scheme as Agent Downer. Her loyalty to her badge or job didn't waver.

She was put in an impossible situation.

We also have to consider that Hera and Zeus might be going about their machinations in a whole new way this time around. It would make sense to change their MO when it gets discovered.

Vanilla leads in an elf by the name of Magenta. The tiny woman wrings her hands together, her shock of white hair dyed the same color as her name, if her roots are any indication. The wrinkles in her features make it clear that she has been working for the Santa Claus family for a very long time. If I was a better man, I might give her a warm, comforting smile, but I know from experience that if I try to be nice, it only ends up looking like I'm glowering. I blame the beard. Not my lack of practice.

"Magenta," Raya begins with a closed-mouth smirk. "Please, take a seat. We only have a few things to discuss with you."

"Thanks, I guess," the elf squeaks. "Did I do something wrong?"

"We're meeting with all of the workshop's employees and probably everyone in town, Magenta. We have some questions. Nothing to worry about." Raya punctuates her spiel with a grin. "How long have you been working here?"

"About forty years," Magenta answers. "I like the work. It makes me happy to make other people happy."

Raya jots this down. "And have you traveled outside of Christmas Town lately?"

The elf gasps, like leaving is the most ludicrous idea in the world. "I would never leave town." She shoots me an accusatory glare, and I shrug.

"Any visitors hanging around your home?"

And so it goes on for the rest of the day. We interview as many people as we can, all the while keeping a watch over the computer sandwiched between us. Every now and again, Santa waves at one of the cameras to let us know he hasn't forgotten about us.

During our chat with an elf named Frankincense, I glance at the computer, only to see *him*.

My arch-nemesis.

My enemy.

The world's biggest asshole: Santa's son, Niko.

Santa points out the cameras to him, and it's only by the cheesy and sardonic smile on Niko's face that I can tell he knows I'm here.

*Fucking great.*

The second he runs into Raya he'll tell her everything. I don't know why the idea of her knowing about The Incident bugs me so much, but it does.

I barely pay attention or take notes during the rest of Frankincense's interview. I'm too distracted by the eventuality that Raya and Niko will meet. I've got to wonder if he's as charming as he always was. If he is, he might very well try to seduce Raya to prove a point. To prove that he can.

Not that I would care if Niko *did* put the moves on Raya. She's a grown woman more than capable of making her own decisions. It's not like there is anything between us but a tense, *somewhat* professional relationship.

If she falls for the dickweed, that's on her.

I wouldn't feel a damn thing. No jealousy. No anger. Nothing.

"Are you okay?" Raya pokes my arm as Frankincense closes the door behind him. *Oops.* "You didn't listen to him at all. He was talking about the trip he took to Hawaii last month. He's one of the only elves we've spoken to who has left town lately. Apparently, he needed time away from his wife, Vanilla. Gossip is that they hit a bit of a rough patch. Did you really not hear any of that?"

"Sorry," I grumble. "I got distracted."

"Well? Care to explain why you checked out? Was I not asking the questions in the right order? Did you want to complain about something?" The burning look she sends my way makes it pretty damn clear she believes she was handling it all perfectly.

She's right. She is a pro.

"No," is my shining answer. She won't get more out of me. I don't trust myself in this tense moment.

Raya clicks her tongue and crosses her arms. "Could you use more than one syllable to tell me what's going on? Be a reindeer, Klaus. Use your words." Raya turns in her seat to face me, and she leans in very close. "*Communicate.*"

The red of her lips is shocking against her pale face. The hazel of her eyes is so sharp I swear I can feel their *color* rubbing against my beard. The nose ring through her nostril shines at me like a beacon, pulling me in.

"No," I insist through gritted teeth. I'm not talking to her but to myself. I'm trying to warn myself off of Raya.

She's a noob with way too much energy and something to prove. I'm a salty mother fucker who wants to be left alone.

"Say," Raya inches forward. The peppermint hot chocolate she had earlier makes her breath nearly irresistible. "More." A couple more centimeters closer.

Her mouth is *right* there. I swallow hard as I look down at her delicious lips.

I'm not too sure how it happens.

One second, Raya is sitting a foot away from me. The next, I've pulled her onto my lap and my mouth is fused to hers.

I half expect her to push me off and away, to slap me and rage out.

She doesn't.

The batty chick actually runs her tongue along the seam of my mouth with a moan. Her fingers tangle in my hair as she moves her lips against mine. The embrace tastes like candy canes: sweet with a bite.

My heart thunders in my ears as I explore her mouth with my tongue, drawing out the kiss.

I don't want it to ever end.

The second it's over I'll have to explain what the hell happened. For now, I'll sink into it. Sink into Raya.

"Klaus," she whispers against my lips. "I think we need a break from the small room. Maybe get some air before we do something *really* dumb."

"Yeah." I help her to her feet before leaving her alone in the security office.

I don't bother closing the door behind me. I've got a feeling no physical barrier will ever protect me from the way Raya makes me feel.

## 9

### RAYA

The computer blinks to life as I plop into one of the uncomfortable chairs. The screen fills with the footage of Santa's office. The local officers from CTPD who had the night shift assured me that nothing went wrong during their watch.

The wreath is still in its case.

The missing element to this little scene? My partner.

Klaus is nowhere to be found.

I'd bet my echolocation skills that the man is freaking the fuck out after our kiss yesterday.

I haven't seen him since.

Truth be told, I'm pretty confused about the whole thing. Klaus is hot as sin with his long hair, beard, and grumpy attitude. That's not the issue.

The problem is that I am on a mission. I need to be flawless in my agent work.

How can I do that if I'm obsessing over one single kiss?

The simple answer: I can't.

I have to put Klaus Thorsen and his dumb perfect mouth out of my mind and focus on the task at hand.

So what if he's late? That's on him.

*I am a professional—unlike his kiss-giving fine ass.*

I won't do like Vera and fall for the dude I'm working with. I'll be better than her.

"Morning," Klaus grumbles as he finally walks into the security office. He places a white and red travel cup on the desk and a crinkly brown paper bag patterned over with gingerbread cookies and boughs of holly. "That's a peppermint latte. For you. Cookies, too." He runs a hand through his hair before shrugging out of his parka, avoiding my eyes as if I were a gorgon.

"Thanks," I say, digging into one of the still-warm sugar cookies. "You didn't have to do that, but I appreciate the gesture."

Klaus's only response is a grunt. He drags his chair farther away from me before settling into it, arms crossed and stare fixed anywhere but on me.

With a heavy sigh, I kick his boot with mine. "Is this how it's going to go from now on? You kiss me and then ignore me?"

Finally, he looks up at me, brows knitted into his hairline. His cheeks are red as Santa's suit under his beard, but Klaus remains silent.

"Reindeer caught your tongue?" I tease, nudging him with my boot again. "Maybe we need to clear the air after—"

"No," he grumbles.

"Yes," I insist.

If any other man had kissed me without explicit consent, I'd be nailing his balls to the wall while singing a cheerful Christmas song.

*Jingle balls, jingle balls, jingle all the way.*

But the thing is I don't mind that Klaus kissed me. I'm not entirely sure if he pulled me into his lap or if I leaped onto him.

He's a little bit distracting, and that is the *only* reason why I want to discuss this whole kiss situation. To make sure it doesn't happen again.

"Look, drink your latte and get ready for another day of interviews, okay? As far as I'm concerned? That kiss never happened."

My jaw drops down onto the table while my back straightens. *Forget it ever happened*? Is he for real?

There isn't a gingerbread cookie's chance in Christmas Town that I will ever forget that kiss.

It was way too damn good for that. His beard left red scratch marks on my cheeks that I can still feel tingling. His lips were soft and firm, moving perfectly to the right rhythm.

If Klaus can sit there and pretend we never kissed, then surely I didn't make enough of an impression on him.

That annoys me more than his monosyllabic conversation skills.

Without thinking too much about what I'm doing and why, I push away from the table and stand, only to straddle Klaus into his chair.

"What are you doing?" he asks. His hands grip my hips tight, keeping me locked in place. He might not know what I'm doing, but he doesn't want me to budge an inch.

"I'm proving a point."

And then, I lock my fingers into the hair at his nape and fuse my mouth to his on a long, searing, snow-melting kiss.

The gentle graze of his beard on my skin.

The firm movements of his lips on mine.

The strong hold of his hands on my ass.

All of it will be *impossible* to forget. I make sure of it, going so far as to grind against his growing erection. If I started this whole make-out session to prove a point, my goal changes pretty quickly.

I don't want to kiss Klaus so that he never forgets how good it is.

I kiss him because I *want* to. Because I *need* to. Because it is the most delicious thing I've ever done in my life.

The man might be monosyllabic, but he *knows* how to use his tongue just fine. He rubs it against mine, exploring my mouth, alternating between smooth sips of my mouth and deep explorations that make my core clench and flutter in anticipation.

"Raya," he groans against my lips. "What on Santa's red sleigh are we doing?"

"Kissing," I respond before diving for his mouth again.

He moans, cupping my face as he nips my lower lip. "I know *that*. We shouldn't."

"You said our kiss never happened. I wanna make you know that not only did it happen but you won't be forgetting about it any time soon."

He leans away from me, his hands traveling down my arms to rest on my hips. The corner of his mouth quirks up with the hint of a smirk. "And why would you want me to remember the kiss?"

"Because," I whisper, leaning into him once more. I'm taking a page out of his book and only responding with one-word answers.

The truth is I don't want to tell Klaus why I wanted to kiss him or why it's important to me that he never forgets it.

If I try to explain my reasoning, I won't like what I find.

Probably a very inconvenient attraction to an emotionally unavailable grouch who hates Christmas, heights, and communication. Three things that are kind of important for a bat shifter.

Okay, maybe not the *Christmas* of it all, but the rest sure is essential to me.

Heights? I am a winged creature who flies for fun.

Communication? I am a gifted echolocator, but those skills don't exactly make it any easier for me to read Klaus's thoughts.

"Because of *what*, Raya?" Klaus insists as his fingers draw patterns along my arms.

"We've got work to do." I push off of him and return to my own seat.

Despite my burning cheeks and overheated body, I take a long gulp from the latte and make a big show of eating the cookies. I need to keep my mouth occupied before I devour Klaus again.

Better to eat my body weight in sugar cookies than blurting out, *Take me to the inn and screw me hard and fast seven ways to Christmas.*

That's not professional.

Definitely not behavior becoming of a FUC agent on a mission to make a name for herself.

*Eyes on the prize, Raya. And the prize is* most definitely *not Klaus Thorsen.*

10

**KLAUS**

The last time my balls were this blue I was seventeen and living in this very town as a social pariah.

The reasons were different, of course.

I was a tall, gangly, nervous wreck of a reindeer with a fear of heights and no way to shake my peers' impression of me as shy and awkward Klaus.

Now, I am a grown man.

There is no reason for my condition.

Only, that's not true.

The *reason* is a person.

A saucy, annoying, stubborn, sexy, pain-in-the-ass, hilarious batty lady.

Raya didn't simply *kiss* me in the security office two days ago. She somehow found a way to weasel her way into my thoughts, under my skin. I swear to Frosty, every time I take a breath, I can hear her voice teasing me for my monosyllabic ways. Every time she moves in close to me, parts of my anatomy perk up. It's like her presence is MiracleGro or something.

I don't understand the attraction between us. That

powerful, almost *visceral* reaction she elicits in my body, mind, and soul. I've been on the brink of losing my mind over Raya for over forty-eight hours now.

It doesn't help that we spend a lot of our time alone in a tiny room.

Today, we're going over all the interviews, cross-referencing them with personnel files and what we've learned from town gossip. No one has made a move on the wreath. Not one single person, visitor or local alike, has raised any suspicion.

There's only one person I've got any bad vibes for.

Niko.

I'm not an idiot. It's entirely due to our personal history. My feelings have no real foundation in truth. If Christmas Town wants to crown Niko the Psycho as their next Santa, that is *their* business. Not mine.

Raya sighs, pushing away another file before rubbing her eyes. "I'm gonna say something. It'll sound insane and unprofessional, but lemme get it out."

I arch a brow at her, waiting for her to go on.

"Vitality Holdings is run by Lisbeth Bannon, right? And we know that either she *is* Hera or she is being *controlled* by Hera. The Zeus dude, we've got no possible link. These people are after anything that will grant them immortality. They tried to get their hands on the Bloody Doctor's research. When that fucked up, they went for the plant genome. They were caught again, and what? Now they're literally chasing myths like the Holy Grail? Are they also roaming crop circles in the hopes of finding aliens?"

"Are you gonna get to your point?"

Raya shrugs. "That's just it. There is no point. We came here on the off chance that these Hera and Zeus lunatics will come here to find the Holy Grail. Problem is we have no tangible proof that they'll come here."

"That's why T-Bone and Director Cooper have other teams keeping watch on the other stuff. Crop circles included," I add with a grin.

Her jaw drops after a gasp. "Did you make a joke? An actual *funny* joke? Who are you, and what have you done with Klaus?"

"Stop," I plead. "It won't happen again."

"But it should. That was good."

I smirk because there's nothing else to do. When Raya Slaski beams at you like you've got sunshine coming out your ass, you smile. It's basically a law.

"We should pack it in for the day, or we'll be late for dinner with your parents. Not to mention, we need to clean up all of these cookie crumbs before the local PD gets here." She points to the morsels decorating the front of my black tee.

"Too late," Officer Wassail Sugarplum says, coming into the small security office. "I'm already here."

"Hey, Wassail," Raya greets him with a warm grin. "How's it going?"

He raises his cup of hot chocolate to her. "Can't complain. Lots to do, of course, but that's to be expected this time of year. You two have anything to report before you head off?"

"No," I answer. "Did you manage to get us that list of all the vendors?"

Wassail nods and drops a thick file onto the table. "It took some doing, but we managed. What you've got here is a list of every single company or vendor Christmas Town does business with. The only ones missing will be the ones Santa uses."

"I'm getting that list from Santa," Raya reminds him for the millionth time.

Really, Wassail isn't a bad cop. He's just a bit on the complaining side. He's always got something to gripe about. It's as annoying as it is endearing for a man who should've retired a decade ago. Thing is, it's excessively difficult to find people who want to live in Christmas Town. Unless someone is born here or marries into a local family, it's almost impossible to get people to move here.

Not because no one wants to.

Rather, the vetting system is intense.

That's why Raya and I have decided that if there is a mole in town, it might be one of the vendors who do business here.

It was actually Raya's idea.

The woman isn't merely sexy as hell. She's way smarter than me. Not that I will *ever* admit this to her.

---

I DON'T KNOW what to do with this sight.

Raya Slaski is standing in my parents' kitchen, rolling cookie dough into neat little balls before placing them on a large baking sheet. She sways to the Christmas music playing on the small radio, singing about every third word under her breath.

It's strange to realize that she actually fits in here, making my mother's famed sugar cookie chocolate balls.

She belongs here way more than I do.

"Do you think the furnace is okay?" she asks, grabbing more dough from the huge ceramic bowl. We'll be balling for hours yet.

"I think there's nothing wrong with the furnace," I answer.

Raya frowns, but it only takes her a couple seconds to understand. "They're trying to give us space."

"Something like that."

About fifteen minutes ago, once dinner was all cleared away, Raya and I started helping my parents with the Christmas baking. Dad heard a mysterious sound coming from the furnace room at the back of the house. Moments later, he called my mother over to help.

There's nothing wrong with the heating system.

My folks are definitely not as sly as they think they are.

"So, what?" Raya wiggles her brows. "They want us to get all chummy while making cookies?"

"Something like that," I repeat.

"Have they met you?" She snorts on a giggle. "You're not an easy dude to know."

I don't respond because she's right. Though Raya knows more about me than anybody else outside of Christmas Town, I don't say that aloud. Not because I'm ashamed.

It's more of a saddening realization.

After what happened with Niko and his band of idiots, once the whole town took his side, it was easier for me to pretend that the town was a bad place full of shitty people.

I brought that pain with me into FUC, and since then, I've had a really hard time trusting people.

In a lot of ways, I see the world in the very same way as Christmas Town. A crappy place full of crap people.

And this cheerful holiday thought is brought to you in part by childhood trauma.

"I'll crack you, you know," Raya announces. She breaks one of her sugar cookie balls in two to demonstrate her intention. She pops one of the halves into her mouth with a devilish, mischievous grin. "I've got the skills it takes."

Thing is I believe her. Not only because she is a competent agent.

The more time I spend with her, the more I *want* her to know me.

That's... *surprising.*

It's actually downright shocking, especially since I know a lot about her life. She's told me all about her parents and her perfect sister. Her failed university career and her obsession with leather jackets.

I'm developing my own obsession with her coats.

"You can try to crack me all you want, Raya. Doesn't mean it'll happen."

"Oh, I've got my ways." She winks at me, and I nearly swallow my tongue.

Raya takes a few steps toward me, wiping her hands on her reindeer apron. Her hand, that small, warm weight, falls onto my shoulder. "I'll get to the gooey center of you, Klaus Blitz Thorsen."

And at that moment? I want her to do just that.

## 11

## RAYA

*My hand is on Klaus's shoulder. Brimming blood bag. What a shoulder it is.*

I knew he was muscular, but this is next level. I pat him for good measure, and not at all because I don't want to stop touching him. Klaus grins, the smile barely making it through his beard. It shines in his eyes, pulling a shiver out of me. He really is a good-looking man.

No, that's too simple.

He's his own category of hot. He's not simply tall and muscular with tattoos and long hair like he waltzed out of those rock music magazines I used to read from cover to cover three thousand times every day as a kid.

He's got this whole other quality about him. It lies under the surface, only appearing in little flashes. Like when his mom handed him a frilly green and red apron and he didn't even hesitate to put it on. Like when she asked him for a hug, and he complied. Like when it became clear to me that, though Klaus hasn't seen his parents in years, he hasn't forgotten the sugar cookie recipe his mother is famous for.

He knows it by heart.

"You might think you're an international, supernatural man of mystery, but I'll figure you out." My voice comes out all breathy.

Klaus takes a step forward, one of his hands going to my hip. His long, strong fingers caress the curve. I forget my name, where we are, and what we're doing. I don't know why he's decided to put his hands on me, but I don't ever want him to stop. I want to stay right here for the next eternity or so.

"Raya." My name is a raspy whisper made of naughty things. "You're in danger of doing something we're both going to regret."

Either I've lost the plot or Klaus is looking at my lips like they're the most delicious thing in existence.

"Oh, yeah? And what am I in danger of?"

"You don't want to know."

"Pretty sure I do."

His breath stutters out of him, and he takes another step forward. I have to crane my head to catch his gaze, and of course, the movement puts me that much closer to him. I lick my lips because the more he stares at them, the more my mouth wants him to do something about it already.

"You don't want this," he murmurs.

"I really do."

My hand is still on his shoulder, relishing the flex of his muscle. My body thrums with anticipation.

This moment is leading to a kiss.

It has to.

Klaus cups my cheek with one large hand, his thumb drawing a line across my lower lip. "Did you know that your lips are red like cranberries?" If he was expecting a response, he won't get one. I'm too stunned to speak. "It's the strangest, most mesmerizing thing in the world. You don't even have lipstick on. It's natural. It's impossible to resist doing this..."

He steps forward, his body towering over me. With my cheek in his hand, he tilts my face up to him. His eyes are burning with a desire I recognize.

*He is going to kiss me.*

And he does.

His lips brush against mine gently. The coarse hair of his beard is in direct opposition to the softness of his lips. He places another kiss on my mouth before letting his tongue run the seam, teasing, tasting, almost testing my reaction.

I won't back down.

I can't. I don't want to. The only thing I want at that moment is to devour Klaus or, at the very least, let him devour me right back. I wrap my arms around his neck, using his height to hoist myself up an inch or two off the ground. I crush my breasts against his chest as I delve my tongue into his mouth, exploring him. He moans, his fingers tightening on my cheek while his other hand cups my ass. He brings me into him, leaving little to the imagination.

His erection presses into my side, and I groan because we're in his parents' kitchen, on a mission. We don't have time to kiss like this, to make our way to the first available surface to chase that blissful oblivion.

Yet, a big part of me wants to throw caution to the wind and do just that.

"Raya," he moans against my lips. "You're the noob who has more sense than a loose-cannon loner like me. You should push me away right now. Give me shit for even deigning to put my hands on you."

"I want your hands on me. I also want *my* hands on *you.*"

"You're supposed to be the one with good sense."

"Exactly," I quip before kissing him again.

"Oh!" Holly's gasp pulls me right out of the moment.

I leap out of Klaus's arms, and he turns toward the counter to adjust his situation below the belt. His mother is frozen in place.

"I'm so sorry," Holly stammers. "I didn't mean to interrupt, dearies. I didn't think you two were... That's to say... Patridge, get in here."

Klaus frowns. "Let's not make a big deal out of this."

Holly raises a brow at him. "Oh, we're not going to make any sort of fuss about our son kissing his partner in our kitchen. None at all. We're going to continue making cookies like nothing happened."

And that's exactly what we do.

Holly shoots me sideway glances the entire time we continue our baking tasks. It continues as we clean up and put our work away. When Holly hugs me goodbye, asking me to come back again soon, she whispers in my ear, "He's a good man. He's been hurt. Be patient, Raya."

It stuns me into silence. I don't know what to do with the information. The only thing I *do* know is that I like kissing Klaus, and I definitely don't know how I'll make it another few days without kissing him again and again and again.

---

THE WALK back to the Jingle Bell Inn is quiet. In fact, Klaus has barely said a word to me since his mother found us dry humping and kissing each other like horny teenagers.

I can't tell if he's embarrassed we were caught or if he regrets it. If we weren't on assignment in his hometown, I would let it go. I would wait and see what happens.

I can't.

"So it seems that we can't be left alone anywhere we go."

Klaus chuckles softly but doesn't respond. I am seriously starting to doubt the zoologists who claim reindeer are sociable and chatty animals.

"It really does look to me like you can't get enough of my cranberry kisses." I purse my lips at him as a joke, grabbing his arm to stop him from walking away.

The hint of a smirk melts his glower.

I continue pouting at him as I step toward him. It's cold out here, but I'm sure we can find an activity to keep each other warm. I raise myself up to the tips of my toes and press my lips to his furry cheek.

His hands grab my hips, but he doesn't make another move. "Raya," he warns. "What the hell are you doing?"

"I'm tempting you with my cranberry lips. I should think it was obvious. Maybe I need to be more straightforward." Without further ado, I kiss him square on the mouth, my tongue dipping between his lips like a shy little turtle.

It takes him only a second to react. He holds me closer, his lips moving in time with mine. I was right, of course. I don't feel the cold at all anymore. All I can feel is Klaus's arms around me, his feverish kisses, and his hands traveling everywhere he can reach. I want to curse my leather jacket for the first time in my life. Usually, I love it. I use it like armor, but right now, my favorite garment is in the way.

"We really need to figure out what's going on here." He sighs without letting me go.

"We're on the mission, Klaus. First, we'll figure out if someone really is after the wreath."

He shakes his head. "Not what I was referring to. I meant between us. We need to figure out what the hell is happening between us. We can't keep kissing whenever we find a free second."

I roll my eyes. "I know that. Do you think I *want* to want

you? Hell, no. My sister met her boyfriend on her first assignment. I don't want to follow in those footsteps. Everyone will think I'm copying her *again*."

Klaus arches a brow. "You really think that's the biggest concern right now? What your family will think?"

"Sort of?" I blush all the way to my toes.

"You really take sibling rivalry to a whole other level, Raya. You should be concerned that it will distract us from our work. That Alyce will be pissed."

"Director Cooper won't say a thing about it. It's not like she would believe it, anyway. Her loner-est loner to ever loner? Kissing his partner? She'll laugh herself silly."

"Loner-est isn't a word."

"It is when it comes to you, Blitz." I wink because I'm joking and totally trying to rile him up. If he's mad, he doesn't even show it. In fact, the dude is still holding me.

In the end, I get what I want.

A kiss.

**12**

---

## KLAUS

Why I'm still holding on to Raya is a damn mystery.

I command my arms to drop, but the stupid things don't listen. It's not like I really want to let her go, anyway. If I had it my way, we wouldn't have been caught in my parents' kitchen. We would have been in one of our rooms, naked and panting. Instead, we had to go through the awkwardness of cleaning up the kitchen with my mom giving me all kinds of looks.

She was already planning my wedding to Raya.

That wasn't where this—whatever was happening between Raya and me—was going.

Neither one of us wants a relationship. At least, not that I know. Raya is new to the FUC, and she's also very well aware that I don't play well with others.

That I can't seem to keep my hands—and lips—to myself is a whole other issue.

"Maybe we need to establish some rules to make the rest of this mission run smoother."

"By smoother," she quickly replied, "we need to stop tearing at each other like a pair of hormonal teenagers?"

I chuckle. "Yeah. Something like that."

"I've never really been a fan of rules."

I grin, because what else am I going to do? Call her out on it? Unlikely. Besides, from what I know of Raya, she's right. She strikes me as the rule-breaking type. Not that there is any sort of precedent about agents bumping uglies.

Not that I think for two seconds that Raya's bits are uglies.

I bet my left nut they're lovely.

*Wait a damn minute.*

Did I just really think that? What the hell is wrong with me? I shake my head, still reluctant to drop my hands from Raya's curvy hips. I need to step away from her and make better decisions. As the senior agent, it should be my duty to put an end to this. We need to focus on Vitality Holdings and the possibility that they've infiltrated the town to get their hands on the wreath.

We can't focus on what we could do to each other naked.

*There I go again.*

"Let's go skating," I blurt out.

Raya laughs. "Why? What does skating have to do with anything?"

"Not a fucking thing, but it's a public activity that still gives us the freedom to talk. We need to strategize, but if we go to the inn right now, I make no guarantees that I won't try something."

*Shut your mouth, Klaus.*

Raya's eyes spark with interest. "Oh?"

"Keep it in your pants, Slaski. We can't go there. The whole purpose of going to the skating rink is so we'll keep our hands off each other."

She smirks like she has other plans, the saucy bat. "Sure. We can do that."

The Christmas Town skating rink is near the center of town and the majority of stores. Our walk over takes less than ten minutes. The rink is owned and operated by a local family. The Partridges. You cannot make this shit up. That's their name.

We grab skates and settle on the red-and-white-striped benches to lace up. Christmas songs play from the loudspeakers, and massive candy canes line the wooden boards painted to look like a gingerbread house. Just like everything else in Christmas Town, the holiday exploded on the decor.

"I can't remember the last time I skated," Raya says as she makes her way to the ice, wobbling on her blades. "I remember it being easier. I guess I had less fear as a kid. You know how children are. Those wee fuckers can get away with doing a bunch of stuff that seems to get scarier as your self-preservation skills develop as an adult."

I make a noncommittal sound because I was never one of those fearless kids. That's one of the main reasons why I can't stand to be in Christmas Town. It brings up too many bad memories of all the teasing.

"I like to skate," is what I choose to respond.

Raya giggled. "Of course you do. You gonna tell me why you hate it here now?"

"Nope."

The second my skates hit the ice I bolt. I put all of my speed into my movements, skating with ease around the rink before coming back around, stopping beside Raya.

"Showoff," she grumbles, still trying to move a few feet without pausing.

She almost falls in a dramatic hand-flailing gesture that has me bursting out laughing.

I don't remember the last time I did that. *Laughed.* A real, honest laugh.

"Don't mock me, Blitz," she warns, pointing her mitten at me. "It's not nice."

"I wouldn't dare. Come on. I'll help you." I take her hands in mine and turn to skate backward, dragging her along with me. I give her a few tips on how to move, but she's too stiff to listen.

She's scared of falling, and I've got to say I can't blame her.

"We're supposed to be discussing our assignment, but I can't focus like this. I'm gonna break my face."

"We can't have that." I chuckle. *Because then how would I kiss you?* I try to push the thought away, but it doesn't budge from my mind. In fact, the more I try to *not* think about kissing Raya, the more my brain demands just that.

I ease us to a stop, placing my hands on Raya's hips to steady her. Is it a lame-ass excuse to touch her? Yes. Most definitely. I lean down and rub my lips against hers in the barest hint of a kiss.

"I'm pretty sure that's counter-intuitive to what we're trying to do here."

"I know."

"We don't even like each other," she grumbles.

I guffaw. "I like you fine. In fact, I like you more than most people I meet."

"Then maybe what I should have said is, I don't like *you*." Her gaze is bright, her cheeks crimson, and though she tries *not* to smile, she's failing. I can *sense* her teasing.

"You don't like me?"

"Nope. Not even a bit."

"Hmm." Well, that won't do. I know she's kidding, but I don't like it. I want Raya to have nothing but good - if not *naughty* - feelings for me. If only I knew why that urge is all-encompassing. "What is it you take issue with, Agent Slaski?"

She narrows her eyes, that smirk still tugging at her delicious lips. "For one, your jackass reputation. Then there's your fear of heights. And, of course, the whole story behind why you left home and why you haven't come back. Oh, and why you hate Christmas, of all damn holidays to hate."

"Is that all?"

She takes a moment to consider this. "No. I don't like that you do sweet things out of nowhere. Like bring me lattes and hot chocolates. I don't like that you remembered your mother's cookie recipe by heart. It makes it very hard to keep hating you."

I chew on the inside of my cheek, trying to keep the admission to myself, but it's too late. It's the only thing my mouth wants to say.

"I make those cookies every year at Christmas. I typically bribe the kitchen staff at whatever hotel I'm staying to let me use their tools and oven."

Raya gasps. "What? Why?"

I shrug. "I miss home too, sometimes. Or I miss my parents."

"Then why not visit?"

"Because there's a lot of history here. Not all of it is good. I've offered to pay for my parents' trip to wherever I was, but their answer was always no. If it's not Christmas in Christmas Town, they want nothing to do with it."

"I guess I understand how that would disappoint you a bit."

I run a hand back through my hair. "Their jobs here are more important."

She frowns and wraps her arms around my waist.

"That's bullshit, Klaus. Your parents adore you. Whatever it is that has come between you all, you need to fix it. Clear the air. I bet then it won't seem like a slight to you that they don't want to leave town for the holidays."

Whatever I want to respond gets stuck in my throat.

"There's one more thing I really don't like," Raya whispers after a too-long silence.

"Oh?"

"How damn irresistible you are." She smirks, and I could kiss her for changing the subject right when I needed it.

"Let's get back to the inn. We'll do hot cocoa and mission planning."

And at that moment, I really meant it.

Other parts of my anatomy had different plans.

13

———

**RAYA**

I pace the length of my room for the millionth time since we got back ten minutes ago. Klaus went to his own room to change, and the plan is to meet back here in a few minutes to *actually* go over our assignment.

Or more to the point: how the hell we're going to *stop* kissing.

I'll be the first to admit that going to the skating rink was a bad idea. Not because I am a terrible skater, though that's still true.

It was a mistake because it was very much a date activity. Everything about it felt like a date.

I can't date Klaus.

He's a notorious lone reindeer who typically communicates in monosyllabic sentences. It's common knowledge that he usually spends his holidays on a beach with a half-naked hottie.

That doesn't exactly scream *well-adjusted adult who is ready for a relationship with a fellow agent.*

To be fair, Vera started dating her jack-o-lantern-shifter boyfriend when he was under her protection. At least Klaus would be a step up from Jack. But he's a botanist who did a cute thing by creating a blood supplement for Vera. The man knows she can't bear to ingest blood, so he fixed up something for her. That's romantic, in its own creepy shifter way.

Klaus doesn't strike me as the cute type.

Even if he did admit to making his mother's cookies every year because he missed her.

*Must not find the hunking hunky hunk sweet. There lies danger, Raya.*

A soft knock on the door makes me jump right out of my thoughts.

I open the door to let Klaus in, confused by the tray he's holding. It's loaded down with two cups of hot cocoa and a mound of cookies.

"This town is really into its sweets."

He chuckles. "Yeah. I don't know how much flour they have to import, but I'd bet it's one of the busiest vendors."

I nod. "Then I should definitely look into them. You know. For the mission."

"The mission. Right. That thing."

Klaus sets the tray down on the little coffee table. The room is small, and he seems to fill it up completely with his tall and muscular form. The only place to sit is my bed because *of course* it is. He eyes it nervously, but I click my tongue in annoyance.

"Relax already. You're making me nervous."

He fidgets into place before running his hand back through his hair. "I guess coming to the rooms was a bad idea."

"I'd say so, yes."

"Raya, what the hell are we doing? What's going on? Because I'll be real honest with you here. I am really confused. One second I wanna strangle you for being so... *you.* Then next, I want to throw you over my shoulder and have my way wicked way with you because you're so..."

"Me?" I offer.

His throat works on a swallow. "Yeah. Exactly. Explain that to me, will you?"

"Would that I could, Blitz."

"We couldn't stand each other a few days ago. What the hell changed?"

I sit beside him because, really, as baffled as he is, I'm right there with him. "I don't really know. We got to know each other. Interacted."

"Right. Before that, all I knew about you is that you're a new agent who is related to Mila, the Bloody Doctor, and the agent who put me on that plane."

I have to work hard to stifle my laugh. The man really doesn't like heights.

"All I know about *you* is that stellar reputation of yours. I was scared that you'd fuck this up for me. I need to do a good job to prove myself."

"So we both had some pretty shitty information on the other. We didn't *actually* hate each other."

"We didn't know each other," I concur.

"Interesting."

"Isn't it, though?"

"Now that I know more about you..." He lets the rest of his thought drop off. "I wanna know more. Every detail you share brings up twenty more things I wanna know about you."

I roll my lips into my mouth, trying to kill my smile. That's a flattering thing to hear. "I get that. I feel the same. Though you've been a little more tight-lipped."

"I told you. I'm not great at letting people in."

"Then tell me one thing. One thing that you don't want to share because you're scared of how I'll react."

Klaus's jaw clenches as he thinks about it for a moment. He takes so long I start to think he'll keep quiet and leave. He surprises the hell out of me when he places his hand on my thigh.

"Something I'm scared to say because of your reaction," he repeats. "How about this. I want you, Raya."

My jaw drops, and my eyes nearly pop right out of my head. "You what now?"

I never did get to hear his answer. The next thing I know, Klaus was kissing me like his life depended on it. He eases me down onto my back, pushing me into the fluffy mattress. One of his hands cups my face while the other goes down to grip my hip to tilt me into his pelvis. His erection digs into my side, and I moan because *sweet hard candy canes.* The man's got a serious package.

"Raya, is this okay?" he asks, peppering kisses on my cheeks, down my neck.

I arch off the bed and wrap my legs around his waist, lining us up in the most delicious way. "What do you think?"

He sighs in relief. "Thank fuck." His hands slide down the length of my body to grip the hem of my shirt. He pulls it off my head and groans when he sees my bra. It's a lacy black number with tiny red cherries on it. "I'm gonna pretend those are cranberries," he whispers, sliding one strap down my shoulder.

"What's with you and the least sexy fruit in the world?"

"It's not. It's the sexiest because it reminds me of you."

*Wow.* If he's dropping that line to get into my pants, it is definitely going to work. It's equal parts sweet and equal parts arousing.

Klaus reaches behind me and unhooks the claps before

slowly easing the garment down my arms. His eyes are glued to my breasts, his breathing erratic. He flicks my hardened nipples with his thumbs, looking about as pleased as can be. I want to make a snarky comment before I combust, but nothing comes to mind.

The monosyllabic reindeer has rendered *me* speechless.

When his mouth closes on one of my sensitive nubs, I find my voice again, moaning his name loud. My fingers tangle in his hair to keep him close to me. I never want him to stop, but I want so much more.

Klaus senses my desire and begins to kiss across my chest, nipping at the tender skin of my breasts. He spends some time exploring the massive bat tattoo wrapped around my ribcage. He continues to kiss his way down my body until he hits my waistband. With agile fingers, he flicks the button open and unfastens the zipper.

I stop his progress, nearly making my lady parts cry out in protest. I fumble with his shirt, and it takes me a few tries to get it off of him. Klaus's entire upper body is covered in tattoos. He is a colorful canvas, and I want to take a moment to inspect each tattoo.

Later.

When I'm not so keyed up I'm seconds from losing my mind.

Both of his nipples are pierced, the barbells twinkling in the dim glow of the lamp. I flick them, and he groans. I smile because it's hot as hell to make a man like Klaus react so powerfully with the barest of touches. We continue stripping out of our clothes until we're nakedly exploring each other with fingers and lips.

"We don't have to go any further," Klaus whispers against my ear.

"Are you kidding me?"

He chuckles. "I'm trying to be a gentleman here, Raya."

I scoff. "A gentleman would give me an orgasm or two before suggesting we stop."

He grins, one brow dramatically arched.

I point toward his impressive erection. "Besides, I'm pretty sure he's gonna have a temper tantrum if we don't get to the good stuff soon."

Klaus laughs, his head thrown back. His hair, free from its tie, is a curtain around us. He looks so carefree, so unencumbered by whatever keeps him sad and locked in a perpetual bad mood. I like seeing this side of him. I also *really* like thinking that I'm the only person who has seen this side of Klaus. A silly notion to have, given that we've only recently met—and at work, no less. But the thought melts my insides like ooey-gooey chocolate chips in a cookie fresh from the oven.

"Did you just claim that my dick will throw a temper tantrum?"

"I sure did. Whatcha gonna do about it?"

His smirk turns devilish, and the man does the very last thing I expect him to do. He leaps to the end of the bed, pins my knees to the bed, and takes a slow, teasing lick up my heated core. I arch off the bed with a surprised—and pleased—gasp of pleasure. The wicked man chuckles against me.

"Figured that would shut you up for a second."

"Well, don't stop, then."

He wouldn't be told twice. Klaus returns his talented tongue to the tight bundle of nerves. Swoops and licks, tugs and bites. Every single touch is perfect, driving me closer and closer to the edge. My fingers dig into the bed as I arch my hips up to meet him. He doesn't seem to mind. In fact, it only spurs him on.

When my legs begin to shake, announcing one hell of a powerful release, Klaus dips a finger into my core, curling it up to press *right* where I need him to.

It's all it takes.

I cry out his name. Maybe a few deities, too. I don't know. I lose all sense of time and space. The only thing that exists is Klaus and his tongue, driving me wild. He continues to kiss and lick me as my orgasm ebbs away.

"Remind me. A gentleman would give you *two* orgasms before suggesting to stop?"

"That's correct," he deadpans, settling his body over mine. He produces a condom from somewhere and makes quick work of rolling it onto his impressive equipment.

This is hardly how I thought my first assignment for FUC would go, but right this second, I don't really care.

I can totally panic about it later.

Right now, all I want is to soak up Klaus and the way he makes me feel.

His intense gaze hooks on mine, locking me in a haze of lust and need. His long hair is an untamed mane around us. His pine scent surrounds me.

"Raya," he whispers, his ear brushing against my ear. "I want you."

"Ditto."

"Is that all you're gonna say?"

"Is Mr. Monosyllabic really asking me to *talk* when he's about to be balls deep?"

"Guess not," he answers before kissing me deeply.

"Stop stalling. Gimme what we both want. That enough words for you?"

He chuckles as he lines himself up with my entrance. He slowly pushes into me, his eyes rolling back with a groan. My breath catches as I hold on to his shoulders. My hips move to the rhythm he sets for us. It's exactly what I need. The man knows how to move. With every thrust, he pushes me closer and closer to that blissful edge.

I clench my core around him as my release takes hold of me. I grip his shoulders and let go into that perfect oblivion of pleasure. Klaus increases his speed, his grip on my hips tightening impossibly. His lips find my neck, where he lays open-mouthed kisses feverishly before groaning my name through his climax.

Laying his forehead against mine, he gulps for breath. "One sec." He rushes off to the bathroom but quickly returns, taking me into his arms. "Whoa."

"Whoa, indeed." I giggle.

I fully expect him to grab his clothes and leave. He doesn't. He surprises the hell out of me by tucking my back into his front. "Sweet dreams, Raya," he whispers in my ear.

And surprisingly, I have the best night's sleep in a grumpy reindeer's arms.

## 14

## KLAUS

I've never woken up like this before. Ever.

Raya is sprawled on my chest, our legs intertwined and my arm around her waist, keeping her tucked close into my side. I swallow hard, waiting for the panic to set. Usually, my skin is itchy until I'm on my own again.

That moment of alarm doesn't come.

In fact, having Raya pressed into me after a decent night's sleep feels... *normal*. I'm at peace in an all-new way. I don't want to contemplate it too much. It's downright terrifying to think that not only did I have sex with my temporary partner but I don't want her to leave.

What I *do* want?

I want to hold her a little tighter. Maybe go for another round before we start off the day.

Raya stretches out in my arms with a cute morning moan. She stills and sits up, her eyes wide and her mouth agape. "Sweet echolocation. We shared a bed."

"We did," I respond, bringing her back to my side. She comes willingly, but not as quickly as I would have liked. "Is that a problem?"

"Not exactly. It was hardly the best idea for our careers."

I shrug. "Shh. Don't ruin the moment with sense."

Raya snorts and pinches my side. "Sense is kinda necessary for our line of work. I think we need to address what happened last night."

With a sigh, I take a second to consider this. What *did* happen? I'm not too sure. "We make a better team than either one of us expected."

"That's an understatement if I've ever heard of one," she mumbles under her breath.

"Is this about your reputation with FUC?"

She doesn't answer, but that's the only response I need. I sit up, bringing Raya along with me until we're reclining against the headboard.

"This morning, we're going to eat breakfast, get ready for work, and hunker down in the security office while we pour over all the vendors that do business with Christmas Town. Once that's done, we will either have a lead or we'll need to find another avenue of investigating."

"What are you doing?" Raya asks.

"I'm telling you what the day is gonna look like."

"I know that. Why?"

"Because that's what we need to focus on right now. We can sit around and dissect what last night meant later when this mission is over."

That might not be the right thing to say, but it's all I've got.

My track record with people isn't great, and though I do trust Raya, there's a new sensation coursing through my veins. I don't know what to call it, but it starts in my chest and radiates out like a hot wave.

The most awkward thing about all this? It's not even *awkward.*

Usually, after waking up next to someone after a night of sex, I can't wait to tow them to the door or make a quick exit.

Despite my puzzled feelings, I know we need to get to work—even if I want to spend the day in bed with Raya.

"So we're putting a pin in this?" Her voice is full of questions, but she settles on the easiest one. "That makes sense," she answers for me. Without another word, she hops off the bed and goes to the bathroom, locking the door behind her.

So much for not being awkward.

***

THE SILENCE IS SO heavy it's damn well near a presence of its own in the small security office. Raya has typed away at the computer for the past three hours, making calls and digging into each vendor that sells its wares in Christmas Town.

For my part, I've been looking into every single person that has married into this loony burg. Thankfully, all of the hotels in town have a guestbook. It makes looking up every visitor that much easier. One by one, I have to remove each patron from the possible suspect list. No simple task, given that we have no real idea as to what we're looking for.

A shifter? A human? Someone who is being manipulated by Hera and Zeus? Maybe one of the shady, shadowy leaders themselves?

Who the fuck knows?

No one, that's who.

I take a gulp of my now-cold latte and wince when the frigid drink hits the back of my throat. A quick glance at the clock tells me that it's nearly lunchtime, but Raya doesn't seem to be least inclined to take a break.

"We should step away from here for a little while. Share what we've found."

Yup. Me. Talking sharing. Christmas Town might as well host a Halloween party.

She arches a brow at me, seemingly surprised that I'm still sitting beside her. It's a jest. All morning, Raya has sent furtive glances my way. Her body keeps leaning into mine, but she always catches herself and overcorrects by drifting so off to the other side that her elbow falls.

"No, thank you. We should keep working. Besides, I think I found something. The flour company? Guess what they're called." Raya can barely sit still in her seat. She's a vibrating bat, drumming her fingers on the desk.

"No idea."

"Olympus Flour."

I frown, but my gut clenches. "Olympus," I repeat.

Raya nods. "It's a little bit too obvious for my taste. It couldn't be Zeus and Hera, could it?"

I lean back in my chair and cross my arms to ponder for a moment. "I don't know. That's a very good question. It's not like these people expected to be found out when Val Downer's blackmail situation was exposed."

"Right. So this could very well be a lead on Vitality Holdings."

"We need to check it out, that's for sure."

With a roll of her shoulders, Raya starts typing furiously on the computer. "I'll get Jessie to look into Olympus Flour's finances."

"Good idea."

Truth is, were this any other case, we would have been the ones to do the digging. This *isn't* a run-of-the-mill case. Not even by FUC standards.

We already know that Vitality Holdings uses some pretty shady techniques to do their dirty work *and* stay under every single radar out there, human and shifter alike.

Last time I spoke to Director Cooper, the identity of Vitality Holdings' owner was still murky. Raya's sister, Vera, and her gourd of a boyfriend learned that the top of the pyramid was *possibly* Jack's ex, Lisbeth Bannon.

Not a conversation I would ever want to have.

*Sorry, honey. Didn't know I was fucking an absolute psycho prone to rule over the world.*

No, thank you.

That's the danger of letting people in. Once you trust them, they can do all kinds of damage. Not that I'm saying I've let Raya in.

So we've had sex.

Kissed a few times.

So she's met my parents.

The fact that I can't help but think about her, even when she is sitting right beside me—after a naked night in the same bed—means nothing.

She still doesn't know why I left home. That's a good barometer for how I feel about this woman. So long as I don't share too much, then I know I'm safe.

From her.

From falling for her.

From the inescapable possibility of heartache and betrayal.

"Well, Jessie is on it. She's gonna get back to us as soon as she finds something."

"She usually—"

"If it isn't my two favorite agents," Santa bellows cheerfully, walking into the security office, effectively cutting off my reply to Raya.

I try to give her a sly look to warn her that she shouldn't divulge our newest possible lead, but Raya isn't even paying attention to me. Her eyes are big and bright, and I swear she hasn't been this excited since she was a little girl who got to sit on a mall Santa's lap.

It's endearing because Raya is adorable.

It's also annoying as fuck because I want to warn her.

"Hey, sir," she gushes. "I mean hi, Mister Santa." Raya might continue to blubber if I don't intervene.

"Nik." I give him a curt head nod, and Raya shoots me a grateful smirk. "Hope you're all ready for the big day. It's coming in fast."

*Small talk? Really?* Who in the fuck have I become?

"The missus and I got to talking last night, and she's dead set on having you over for dinner tonight. I won't take no for an answer."

"We'd love to," Rays squeals excitedly just as I grumble, "No, thanks."

The glare she aims at me is downright glacial. She turns to beam at the big man, smiling brightly. Figures that Raya the Badass would turn into a polite guest because Santa invites her over for dinner.

I want to tell her that she wouldn't be missing much, but really, that would make me a massive dick.

Raya doesn't have to be wary of these people. Not like me. It's not like they'll hurt her like they hurt me. They don't have the right ammunition for that.

At worse, I can find a reason to back out before tonight comes.

There's not a hot chocolate's chance in Santa's workshop that I'm going to dinner. With my luck, they'll invite Niko, too.

As far as I know, murder isn't allowed anywhere.

Least of all Christmas Town.

## 15

## RAYA

Klaus tried to bail on dinner, the big jerk.

I'm not sure what happened to make Klaus hate this town and its people so much, but whatever *did* happen also involved Santa.

*Santa.*

Of all people to hate.

It's so on-brand for Klaus. It's not like I was going to let him get away with it. If I got the man to eat a few dinners with his parents, I *knew* I could convince him to break bread with Santa.

I managed it.

I'm not *proud* of what I did—the bribe I used to get Klaus to come with me. I'll deal with it later. For now, all I want to do is stare at Santa's house because...

Well.

It's Santa's house.

The place is massive. I'm talking Christmas-castle kind of big. If the four-story log and stone home has under twenty bedrooms, I'll eat my tuque. Every single window and door is decked out in all of Christmas's best friends.

Twinkling lights, decorated boughs, wreaths with huge red bows. The house—if I can ever *call* that—is straight out of a kids' Christmas movie. I'm half expecting a talking reindeer to come out of the woodwork with a sassy line.

"I might *sleigh* you for this," Klaus grumbles under his breath, making me snort in the *most* attractive way ever.

Talk about a sassy line from a talking reindeer.

"You'll be fine. Do you need a safe word? How about you say *tinsel tits* the second you want to leave?" I giggle because there is no way either one of us is actually going to *say* tinsel tits in Santa's house.

"I might do it to embarrass you," Klaus warns as he taps my butt.

I don't know if the gesture is loving or teasing. Perhaps both? Regardless of his intent, I'm here for it. Klaus can touch my ass any time he wants.

"Let's get his over with already," he grumbles, ringing the doorbell.

An instrumental and jingly version of "Santa Claus is Coming to Town" echoes through the night, and I burst into laughter. Klaus rolls his eyes, but I jab a warning finger into his side.

"You behave."

"I didn't want to come," he reminds me.

"Well, now you're here. You will be civil because you represent FUC. If you don't try to be nice, then you can forget that *thing*." I wiggle my brows at him, grinning like I mean it. I don't. The chances that I can resist Klaus now that I know what he's packing—and how he uses it—are slim to none.

He balks. "But you promised."

"Be"—I poke his chest—"Have." I jab again for good measure.

The door swings open, revealing a tall, svelte woman with a perfect shock of white hair expertly braided into a crown. Little poinsettias are artistically arranged into the hairstyle.

"Oh, if it isn't Klaus. By Rudolph, you have grown." She hugs him tight before pinching his cheeks. "You're so handsome. I always knew you'd be back. I told everyone for years now that you couldn't stay away forever." She waves us in before taking our coats and gently placing them on a coatrack in the shape of reindeer antlers. She introduces herself and insists that I call her Doris. *Not* Mrs. Claus. "Let's go straight through to the living room. Everyone is waiting for us."

Beside me, Klaus stills. His jaw clenches so hard I nearly hear his dentist snickering over the money he'll make to repair the damage. If we weren't on the job, I would reach out and take his hand in mine.

I'm not Vera.

I might have boned down with my coworker, but I'm not going to *fall* for Klaus. He's a surly uncommunicative reindeer with a grudge against Santa, who prefers to spend all of his time alone.

Doris leads us into an enormous room, complete with a ginormous fireplace and an even bigger tree. An intricate wooden coffee table sits in the very center of the room, around which two sofas and two plush armchairs are arranged expertly to promote conversation. Doris and Santa must do loads of entertaining in this room.

Santa—or *Nik*, as Klaus would call him—raises his glass to us by way of greeting. A young couple is nestled on one of the sofas, while the other is taken by a man, glaring at the whole room. Most of his ire is cast to the other dude, cooing over his girlfriend. The two *have* to be brothers; they look so much alike. In fact, I *know* they're brothers. I recognize that glow of half-hatred in the younger guy's glower.

Sibling rivalry.

"You remember Nils."

The angry brother barely registers our arrival, too angry to care.

I wonder if that's what I look like when I'm around Vera.

Good gingerbread, I hope not.

It's a little intense and a lot uncomfortable.

"And Niko, of course." Doris gestures to one-half of the couple. "That lovely young lady is Cassie Michaels, Niko's fiancée. They're getting married the day after Christmas if you can believe it."

Cassie gives a timid smile that is so sickly sweet I want to barf. "I've always wanted a Christmas wedding," she explains. "Can you imagine having it here, of all places?" Her earrings, kitschy little red ornaments, jiggle as she giggles. Her whole persona is big on artificial shyness. I'm pretty sure she is *pretending* to blush. Who even *does* that?

"I don't know if I'd want to get married the day after Christmas. Here of all places. Hasn't it made everything more hectic? Not only is it Christmas, but a wedding, too?" I shrug. "I've always wanted to get married on a beach somewhere. My toes in the sand and my wedding dress blowing in the wind."

Cassie's veneer slips a little bit, and though I can't quite put my finger on *why*, I actually like the idea that I've annoyed her. It's a very familiar feeling. It's the same feeling I get when Vera does something perfect that makes me look like the world's dumbest tool.

Maybe I understand Nils a bit more now.

"Klaus!" Niko's exclamation is as fake as his fiancée's joy.

"Niko," Klaus growls.

Actually *growls*. I have to do a double take because I can't believe the man, a reindeer, no less, *growled*. If I was physically close to him, I'd elbow him in the side. Yet one look at his pinched forehead, and the urge is curved. Klaus is *not* happy.

"Good to see you back in town," Niko lies.

"Is it?" Klaus claps back with so much ire it makes the fire crackle.

"Boys," Santa warns.

"No, Dad. It's okay. Klaus was never good at *letting* go." Niko laughs like he's hilarious, but I don't get the joke.

Klaus's reaction makes it pretty damn clear that Niko made a jab. Possibly about Klaus and whatever made him leave town for good.

"Why don't you repeat that?" Klaus's intensity is palpable.

A nervous Doris claps her hands together, her eyes brimming with unshed tears. "You two used to be such friends." She sniffles. "Can't we let the past go? It was a reindeer game. Nothing more."

A nerve in Klaus' neck jumps and twitches. He's about to implode. He forces a smile but gets to his feet. "If you'll excuse me." He vanishes down the hall without another word.

*All of the tinsel tits.*

"I'm gonna go see if he's okay." I mumble a series of apologies as I chase off after Klaus.

He puts on his boots and yanks his jacket off the coat rack, not even bothering to put it on before braving the literal North Pole. I'm not that insane. I take the time to zip my leather coat before running down the long and snowy laneway.

"Klaus, you great big brute. Would you please stop making me run after you?"

He barely turns to look at me. "Go back, Raya. It's not often outsiders get invited to that house. Go bask in it."

"No. You're my partner, and you're upset. I know you won't tell me why because you've got this whole cone of silence about everything. Fine. Don't tell me what happened. But that doesn't mean I'm not gonna have your back."

His steps falter, and he finally stops to look at me. His cheeks are red under his beard, the tendrils of his breath curling around a month. "You're not gonna get me to spill."

"I know." I mean it, too. "I don't need to know what happened *unless* it becomes directly linked to our investigation."

"It's got nothing to do with that and everything to do with Niko being a grade-A douchebucket."

"Let's go. Pretty sure I saw a bar called the Drunken Elf, and I need to check it out."

I don't turn back to see if Klaus is following me. I know he will.

Just like I know that after a few White Christmases—one hell of a strong alcoholic drink—he'll spill all of his secrets.

## 16

## KLAUS

"Good *morning*, partner," Raya shouts, chipper as a turtle-dove in a pear tree.

I grunt out my greeting without looking away from the computer. The screen's glare isn't helping my hangover, but I still have to do my job.

Getting drunker than Rudolph after a failed test flight was hardly my best idea.

I'm honestly embarrassed that merely *seeing* Niko made me angry enough to find solace at the bottom of a bottle. Or three.

I'd be a little less disappointed in myself if I actually *remembered* what happened after Raya and I had a few drinks at the Drunken Elf last night. I don't know how much I drank or what I might've said to her.

One thing is for damn sure; we didn't get to that *thing*. Not because I was drunk. Rather, I didn't actually stay for dinner at Santa's place. I lost my chance at another night in bed with Raya Slaski because I can't let go of the past.

"How you feeling?" She puts a peppermint brownie the

size of my head and coffee on the desk. "That's for you. Should help with the hangover."

"I appreciate it. If I could make one request, please don't be so loud."

She grins at me, shrugging out of her coat. I shove my sunglasses into my hair to get a better view of her. Not that it's professional behavior or anything. I can't help myself. Her nose ring twinkles under the office lights, while her hair is wavy and framing her face like it always does. Her curvy legs are draped in a pair of skintight black jeans tucked into a pair of boots that look good but surely can't be warm enough for the Christmas Town climate.

I'm a jackass for not telling her she needs better outerwear. All because I want to keep ogling her like she's the last piece of sticky pudding at a family potluck.

"Less loud?" Raya shouts before giggling. "Sorry. Last time I do that. I just want to get *some* payback for last night."

I groan. "Shit. What did I do?"

"Oh, you know." She blushed. "You danced on the bar and did a striptease to 'Santa Baby.' It was hilarious."

"I did not."

"Okay, you didn't, but the look on your face is priceless. You didn't do anything bad, exactly. But you're quite a big man. Getting you back to the Jingle Bell Inn all by my lonesome would've been... *interesting*."

"Sorry."

"Don't be. Nils ended up helping me."

Cold fills my gut as the booze from the night before makes its way back up my throat. "Repeat."

"Back to monosyllabic? Uncool."

"*Repeat.*"

Raya rolls her eyes. "Nils came into the bar. It's not like he followed or anything. He was there for a nightcap. Away from his brother. We chatted about good old sibling rivalry while you downed nearly all of the town's alcohol."

The more I learn, the angrier I am. I don't like the idea of Raya getting all close and chummy with Nils. Sure, he isn't Niko, but the man is still a Claus. I can't trust him any more than I can trust Rudolph to be invisible in the dark.

That mother fucker *shines*. At least, he would if he was real.

"Once you were done with your impression of a fish, Nils helped me bring you back to your room."

If Raya notices that I'm upset, she doesn't let on.

"I'm actually really surprised to see you awake so early. What are you working on?" She takes her seat beside me, her shoulder pressing into mine.

*Take* that, *Nils.*

"I'm looking into Niko's comings and goings into town."

Raya gasps before decking me in the shoulder. "Are you insane? You can't think that Niko is the mole."

"Sure I can. Maybe he wants to take over Christmas Town before Daddy Dearest retires. Maybe he wants to sell off the town to the highest bidder so he can retire with that fiancée of his."

She narrows her eyes. "What makes you suspect him?"

"Niko is an ass."

"Well, sure. The whole world knows that the next man in line to be Santa is a jerk."

"He is, though." I ignore her sarcasm. "You don't know him."

"Neither do you," she points out like an infuriatingly sexy vixen. "You *knew* him. Before. A long time ago. People grow up. Change. Make better decisions."

"I don't trust him. If Vitality Holdings has a foothold in Christmas Town, it'll be with him."

"You're wrong. I mean that with all of the love and respect in my heart, but really, you're way off base. You're letting the past cloud your judgment on this."

"I'm telling you. Niko is behind this."

"If anyone in that house was fake and in with Vitality Holdings, my money would be on the fiancée. Cassie. Is that even her *real* name? Think about it. Cassie could be a nickname for a whole bunch of names from Greek mythology. You've got Cassandra. Cassiopeia."

I cross my arms and arch a brow at her. "A bunch? Sounds like only two to me."

She waves me off." You know what I mean. It's *not* Niko. I had a long chat with Nils last night. He told me all about Niko's vision for the town and how he wants to streamline some stuff. Nils is against it. Much more of a traditionalist, the baby bro is. I think he'd much rather be the next in line for the big red suit."

She continues rattling off all kinds of things Nils told her, but I don't listen. I am too hungover to argue. Besides, I feel it down to my bones that something is off with Niko.

"We don't even know if anyone is actually *after* the wreath. We've got *two* solid leads with Olympus Flour and Frankincense."

"The spice?"

"The *elf*," Raya answers with a giggle. "Remember? We interviewed him. He's the elf who went on a holiday to Hawaii. If you want to grasp at straws, look into Cassie. Don't people have to go through very intense vetting before marrying into town?"

"Yeah."

"Good. So you dig into Cassie's past. I'll look into Frankincense while we wait to hear back from Jessie about Olympus Flour."

"I think I should interview Nils and Niko. Separately. Preferably in a torture chamber."

"Seriously, dude. Who hurt you?"

*They did.*

I don't say that. I can't. It would mean admitting a whole bunch of stuff I really don't want to get into. Especially not with Raya.

"You leave those two alone. Until we have solid proof that one of them is doing something nefarious, they're in the clear."

"I'm the senior agent." The second the words are out of my mouth, I regret them. "Raya."

"No. I see how it is. I'm good enough to fuck and to bring you home from the bar. Not good enough to trust with your past or *our* mission." She grabs her coat and slings it on.

A bunch of interjections create a blizzard of white noise in my head. I want to tell her to stay. I want to find the words to explain, but I'm out of practice. I haven't had any sort of relationship in too long.

Anything that comes out of my mouth will be wrong and flawed.

I let her go, knowing this time I'm the one who did the hurting.

## 17

## RAYA

*What an absolute jerk.*

I really don't know why I'm so angry with Klaus as I make my way out of the security office and down the hall. I'm hurt because I took care of him when he needed me, but there's a whole other mess of stuff going on in my heart.

Yup. My *heart*.

I don't like it.

So we slept together once. Kissed a couple of times.

It's not like he's the best I've ever had.

Only, that's a lie because Klaus Thorsen is *definitely* the best I've ever had. More than that, I can't help but feel that if he let me in, we could be really great together.

As a team.

Partners.

Not a *couple*.

Okay. So *maybe* a couple.

I bet Vera will *love* to hear all about how I went on a mission and caught feelings. Then her falling in love with Jack won't be such a big deal because I did it too.

Livid and more confused than an elf trying to untangle

strings of lights, I blaze down the long workshop corridors. I'm so caught up in my anger I don't even notice Nils coming toward me.

"Raya." He smiles shyly. "Think we can talk?"

I blink at him as I try to clear my thoughts. "Nils, hi. What's up?"

His pale cheeks redden, the brown of his eyes darkening. "Not much. I wanted to thank you for last night."

"Walk and talk, Nils. I need to be somewhere."

"Oh. Sure. Can I interest you in hot cocoa? Maybe something to eat? Soak up all the booze?"

"Maybe some other time. I'm actually on the clock right now."

He winces, apologetic. "Right. Well. I'll make it fast. Thanks for letting me vent about my family yesterday. It's not often that I get to talk to someone without fear of reprisals."

"Reprisals?"

"No one wants to be the asshole who hates his family. Especially not when said family is literally the future of Christmas."

"It's okay, Nils. Really. I'm no stranger to sibling rivalry. I still think that you could convince your dad to make you and Niko co-Santas."

We make our way onto one of the cabooses. It's the easiest way out of the workshop, and I have to see an elf about a toy.

"I don't know that I want to put myself out on a limb like that."

"For what it's worth, I believe in you." I smile, hoping that it's as friendly as I mean it to be. Given my mood, I'm not sure the execution is all that great.

"Thanks. Niko has something going for him, though."

"He's firstborn?"

"No. Cassie. His fiancée. The role of Santa isn't given to the firstborn but the first to have an heir."

I snort in disbelief. "You're fucking with me."

Nils shakes his head. "No. It's true. My ancestors saw what succession did to kingdoms and tried something different to stave off some in-fighting."

I laugh because, really, it's hilarious. "Did these people not have families? In-fighting and families go together like..."

"Hot chocolate and whipped cream?" Nils offers.

"Something like that, yeah."

"Cassie and Niko haven't been together all that long. Only a few months. I had a girlfriend. Cookie. We broke up a few months ago. Right before Niko met Cassie, actually. Up until then, everyone thought I would be the next Santa in line."

Completely bypassing the fact that his ex's name is *Cookie*, I tap his shoulder. "I'm sorry. That's a lot of loss. Your lady and your dream job. All at once."

He tries to shrug like it's nothing, but his pain is palpable. "I really don't like Cassie. Probably because I can't stop comparing her to Cookie. Cookie would be such a better Mrs. Claus. Her family even owns one of the bakeries in town. She's *from* here. She gets it. Not like Cassie."

I nod. "Planning the wedding the day after Christmas does seem a little..."

"Like my brother is trying to solidify his claim to the Santa suit?"

"That."

"My parents and all of Christmas Town don't see it that way. They think this wedding is saving us or whatever. You said something last night. It stuck with me. I wanted to know if you really mean it."

I gulp. As much as Klaus was drunk and doesn't recall much of the night, I was pretty shit-faced. I wasn't in shape to give any advice. "Look, Nils. I'm not sure you should give any credence to anything I might have spewed with so much booze in my system."

"No way. You were right. You told me that I have to stop comparing myself to Niko. Live my life for me. Do what makes me happy and stop making all my moves like my life is nothing more than a chess game against my sibling. It's bringing me nothing but pain, and that's no way to live."

I'd be more shocked if Nils told me Klaus took flight like a reindeer in an old-school Christmas story.

"I said that?" Damn. Maybe I need to listen to my own advice.

"You're very wise."

"Well, sure." The caboose comes to a stop, and we leap down. "I struggle with that, too."

"You mentioned that. Yeah. That's why I wanted to thank you. The call you made to your sister last night? It helped me realize I need to make amends with my brother. Stop being such a grinch."

"I called my sister?" I stop in my tracks, grabbing hold of Nils' arm. "Are you sure I called Vera?" I have no recollection of that. What the hell was in those White Christmases, anyway?

Nils answers my questions, but I don't hear him. Frank-incense, the traveling elf, hops off the caboose, looking about as chill as a raw gingerbread man in the oven. He pretends he doesn't see me, but the crimson tint of his cheeks makes one thing obvious.

He is guilty as hell. Of what, I don't know yet. Given that he's at the top of my possible suspect list, I need to find out.

"Duty calls, Nils. Let's catch up soon." Without waiting for his reply, I duck behind one of the massive pillars and sneak a peek around it. Frankincense swings a huge red bag over his shoulder, nearly toppling down from the sheer weight of it.

*What in Santa's beard is he doing?*

I'm about to find out if one of Santa's elves is in league with Vitality Holdings.

*Rudolph, help me.*

---

IF FRANKINCENSE IS A BAD GUY, he is by far the *worst* bad guy ever. He can't sneak around to save his life. He greets everyone he passes by with cheerful holiday greetings. It doesn't seem to faze him that he's literally hauling a bag that could crush him to death.

He slowly makes his way down the main street and tries to throw the bag into a small green sleigh. He fails and tries again. This time, when the bag falls, a few townsfolk spot his distress. With big smiles and bright, cheery cheeks, they help Frankincense place his loot in the sleigh.

They've got no idea what's in the bag.

Neither do I, for that matter. All I've got are some instincts that he's up to something shadier than the Grinch in Whoville.

Frankincense hops into his sleigh and drives the damn thing around the corner. It takes some effort to discreetly chase after him. Running stealthily in calf-high snow as dense as a booze-soaked fruitcake isn't easy.

I'm covered in sweat despite the frigid temperature and a

little more than out of breath by the time Frankincense pulls up to a tiny house on the outskirts of town. The elf struggles to bring the bag inside. It takes him about ten minutes to go ten feet.

"What the hell are you doing?" a voice hisses out of nowhere, invading my hiding spot behind a happy spruce.

I strike the newcomer, only to realize a little too late that it's Klaus. He stumbles back, gripping his throat.

*Tip: do no throat-punch the guy you're into. Hardly good foreplay. Even when you're furious with him.*

"The fuck, Raya," he pants.

"Don't sneak up on an agent. What were you thinking?"

"Umm, that we're partners. I saw you sneaking off with Nils. Then I spotted you sulking and following Frankincense."

"I told you I suspected him," I argue. I'm going to let the whole *but we're partners* thing slide. For now. No point in reminding him that he hardly behaved like a good partner back in the security office. "Hey! Why are you here? Who's watching the wreath?"

"Office Wassail Sugarplum," Klaus responds. "He came in to let me know that Santa removed the wreath from the case last night. He obviously put it back this morning since it was there. But..."

"Why did Santa remove the wreath from its secure spot?" I finish the uncomfortable question for him.

Klaus nods. "That's what I'd like to know."

"You can't seriously suspect Santa Claus of being in league with Vitality Holdings." I can barely get the words out.

"I don't know what to think. The man knows it's under surveillance, but he waits for one of his oldest buddies to be on shift to move it."

"We obviously need to talk to him as soon as we figure out what the damn hell this guy is doing."

"Frankincense? He's harmless."

I snort. "He's up to some really shady shit." I give Klaus a brief rundown of what I witnessed, and the more I divulge, the darker his features become.

"Shit." He runs a hand over his mouth. "I'm so sorry, Raya. I really let my past get the better of me. I thought Niko *had* to be up to something."

"We don't know what Frankincense is up to yet. All we've got is some stolen presents or whatever else is in those bags. Besides, I'm getting the impression that there is a lot of bad stuff happening in Christmas Town."

"What do you mean?" he asks.

Before I can respond, the cabin door swings open, and Frankincense returns to his sleigh. His movements are quicker. That, plus the reduced size of the red bag, tells me one thing. He dropped stuff off in the cabin.

I think the elf is playing Santa. The why of it is still a mystery.

"Follow my lead." I leave our hiding spot and stride over to Frankincense. "What are you doing?"

The elf squeaks out in fright, dropping the big red velvet bag to the ground. The second he spots us he puts his hands up in the air. "Please. Don't shoot."

"Don't shoot?" Klaus grumbles. "We've got no weapons."

The elf heaves a sigh of relief but doesn't lower his arms. "I didn't do anything wrong," he stammers, on the verge of tears.

Klaus grabs hold of the bag and looks inside. He pulls out a round cookie tin, its contents rattling. "What's going on, Frankincense?"

"I'm part of the workshop cookie exchange. You know, the one your parents organize? I'm delivering the goods."

"Damn. Sorry to have scared you, Frankincense. But now that we've got you here, we've got some more questions about your trip to Hawaii."

The elf answers everything and then some.

He isn't up to anything besides wanting some time alone from Vanilla, his *darling* wife.

That leaves Olympus Flour and, as much as I hate to say it, Santa.

## 18

# KLAUS

Raya and I have been in Christmas Town for nine days now. We're no closer to figuring out which cracks Vitality Holdings could use to weasel their way in.

There are a lot, too.

We might have cleared Frankincense from any possible involvement, but our list of suspects hasn't budged.

Olympus Flour. Santa. *Niko.*

That's my list. Raya refuses to believe that Niko is in on it. She would gladly put Cassie on there for good measure, but from the digging she's done on the soon-to-be-bride, there's nothing there. By all accounts, Cassie is a young woman very much in love.

That alone raises all my hackles but not because Cassie has done anything *wrong*. It's her choice of future husband I question. It's not her fault; rather, it's all me and my past with Niko.

"Klaus," Raya gasps. "Watch what you're doing. You're ruining it." Raya bumps me with her hip, moving me away from the massive gingerbread house laid out on my parents' kitchen counter.

From their vantage point at the dining room table, Mom and Dad exchange a hopeful glance. They really think that Raya and I will be something serious. Probably because they've caught us kissing one too many times.

The way my hands always find their way to Raya's hips or shoulder or toying with her hair doesn't help me, either. How can they believe that we're only partners when every time they turn around I'm mooning over Raya?

Raya is hardly an innocent bystander. The woman keeps smacking my ass every time my back is turned.

Maybe one more roll in the snow would set us to rights. Get each other out of our system. Put this attraction between us to rest.

"I'm not *ruining* it," I argue with her, pocking her nose with icing. Raya squeals and takes a step back, only to slam against the counter.

She arches a brow at me. "So help me, Blitz. If you mess with the structural integrity of my gingerbread house and cost me first place, I'll never forgive you."

"I like her." Mom laughs. "She takes these Christmas Town activities seriously."

The *and that means you'll be around more often* is implied. I hear it in the loud silence that follows and the hopeful look she gives Dad.

Truth is there's a reason why I haven't gone back to bed with Raya.

I'm insanely attracted to her, and despite our tense beginning, she is quickly turning into the one person I don't mind spending time with. She's funny and intelligent. She's a capable agent who doesn't think inside the box. She creates her own box and smashes it when she isn't satisfied with the outcome.

It's what she did with her first gingerbread house earlier tonight.

It's also what she's done with my defenses.

"I like you, too, Holly. If your son doesn't come back here for Christmas next year, I will. I'll dominate all of the Christmas Town competitions. Win it all."

"Our door will always be open for you, Raya." Dad beams.

I swear, they're already imagining grandkids running around. If there was ever a flying reindeer, could the offspring of a vampire bat and reindeer be it?

Probably.

What a terrifying thought.

Having a kid who would be all roped into the Christmas Town drama—one who could *fly*—that would be too much for me to bear.

Weird that it's not the idea of a kid with Raya that freaks me out. It's my hypothetical child being bullied that has me all up in a fret.

"Blitzy-boo," Raya coos teasingly because she *knows* I hate it when she calls me that. "Do me a favor and plop a peppermint on each dollop of icing I put on the roof?" She bats her long lashes at me, already knowing that my answer will be a resounding yes.

There isn't much I would deny Raya Slaski. I simply have to make sure she doesn't clue into that.

"Sure thing."

To complete the decorations of the gingerbread roof, we have to stand *real* close together. Her toes are pressed into mine. For whatever reason, I think it's a great idea to help her balance by placing a hand on her hip.

Yup.

Me. My hand on her hip. For balance. Never mind that she can *actually* fly.

To avoid thinking too much about how much I love touching Raya, what it means, and what will happen when this mission ends and we have to make our way back to FUC, I pop a mint into my mouth.

"Hey!" Raya shouts. "Don't eat my construction material."

"Sorry."

She hip-checks me again. "It's okay. I forgive you this time because you're so darn cute. Don't let it happen again."

"I make no such promise. Mint is my favorite thing."

"Right after cranberries," the saucy little bat whispers under her breath.

There's no chance that my parents heard her, but I sure did. Her words spark interest in a southern part of my anatomy. I clear my throat while my eyes flick toward her lips.

They're *right* there, looking more delectable than ever. Forget gingerbread cookies. Keep your peppermint lattes. Shove your nasty-ass fruitcakes where the sun don't shine.

But those lips?

Leave me those lips to savor all night long.

Without even realizing it, I lean over her and brush my mouth along hers. I swallow her gasp before kissing her softly again. Raya drops the bag of cementing icing to the countertop to palm my chest. My hand goes to her cheek, tipping her head up to gain better access to her delicious mouth.

"Klaus," she whispers against my mouth. "I think we need to stop."

"Huh?" I blink, my thoughts clearing.

My parents are no longer at the dining room table. I don't actually *know* where they went.

"Fuck. I shouldn't have done that."

Raya's eyes sparkle as she shrugs. "I don't mind. I enjoyed it. Though, maybe next time you wanna go all hormonal teen on me, maybe wait for us to be in our hotel room instead of in your parents' kitchen."

"Yup." I step away from Raya and out of the kitchen. My fingers tear at my hair with so much gusto I have to pull off my hair elastic to retie my mane into its bun. "I'm gonna go for a walk."

Raya blinks at me as if she were expecting just that. "You do what you need to do to figure your shit out, Klaus. I'm gonna be right here. At least until Christmas." She takes a few steps toward me and taps my shoulder. "I get that it's hard for a lone reindeer like you to let someone in. I feel for you, but there comes a time when you need to decide if you're okay with being alone or if you wanna make a change." Lifting herself up to the tips of her toes, she places a kiss on my cheek.

She might be a vampire bat with an obsession with leather and combat boots, but Raya Slaski fits into Christmas Town more than I ever did.

That says something important, but I don't know what.

"I need to get out of here for a bit." Without waiting for Raya's response, I rush away, barely remembering to grab a jacket on my way out the door.

My feet have a mind of their own. They lead me straight to Tiny Tim's Tavern off the main drag. I grab a stool at the very back of the bar, away from the door and from the revel-makers. It's hardly a dive bar. Those don't exactly exist in Christmas Town, but it does draw a seedier crowd.

By that, I mean the laborers who work in the greenhouses. They literally plant seeds for a living. I order myself a pint of Prancer's Pilsner. The hoppy, bitter taste is perfect for my mood.

"You look like you could use a chat," a deep, jolly voice booms as a large man plops into the seat beside me.

"Nik," I grumble. "Pretty sure I picked this seat to be left alone."

Santa shrugs. "Pretty sure I don't care too much what you want right now, Blitzen."

I wince, and he doesn't miss it. "You never did. No one in this town did. You gonna tell me why you took the wreath out of its case?"

"I wanted to get a good look at it. See what all the fuss is about."

"It put you on the suspect list. Right at the top."

"Wouldn't expect any less. You're thorough. I gotta respect that."

"That's it? That's all the explanation you've got?" I almost wanted him to admit he was behind everything.

"The lore around the wreath is a mystery, kid. It's been in the family for so long even if it *was* the Holy Grail, melted down into a wreath, I wouldn't know. That lore is lost to time. It's not like it matters. If it had the power to grant immortality, the world would look a lot different."

"What happened to the power of stories?"

Santa scoffs. "Stories have power whether they're true or not. If these Vitality Holdings people think they will be immortal if they get the wreath? They'll stop at nothing to get their hands on it. Imagine what they could do with the *power* behind that story. It could change everything."

"It's a lot to put on faith."

"That's what life is. I'm an old man who has the same job as my father and my great-grandfather and so on. Having faith in something? That's kind of the point of life. I believe in what we do in this town. The hope we give people. What do you believe in, Klaus?"

"Not this town, that's for darn sure."

He claps a hand to my back. "You ever gonna forgive this town for what happened?"

"Nope." I gulp down a mouthful of my drink.

"That's too bad. Your parents miss you. The reindeer training team sure could use a Thorsen. You're from good people, Klaus. Good, strong, hardworking people. Your kin always could train my reindeer like nobody's business. You know how to make 'em docile *and* real performers when they drive sleighs through town. It makes the tourists so happy. A real essential part of this place."

"It's not hard work. We literally shift to train them. Nothing to it."

Nik laughs. "Well, sure. Because anyone off the street can just decide to shift into a reindeer one day."

I don't respond but focus on my beer. The old man isn't done.

"I never should have sided with Niko. What he did was wrong. The whole town knew, too. That's why there was a lot of whispering about town when Nils got together with Cookie Trimmings. Everyone and their grandma wanted Nils to take over the mantle after what happened that night. Now? With Niko getting married to an outsider? Things are tense. It's got nothing to do with the wreath. Your bad guys aren't in this town, Blitz. But your past is. Maybe you can try to fix it while you're here. That might have to start with me, so let me say this. I'm terribly sorry for what Niko did. For what his merry little band of naughty boys did. They got coal in their stockings for a straight decade, but I should've stepped in and been a better Santa."

"That's it? You apologize, and it's done? I forget all about it? No matter the scars and fears I still have?"

He has the decency to wince. "If I could find another way to fix it, I would."

"Fix it? Make Nils the next Santa. Forget the old rules. You'll ruin this town if you let Niko and Cassie take over when you retire. He might be your son, but if he can throw another kid off a mountain as a seventeen-year-old with no real power? What the hell is he gonna do when he has a whole town at his beck and call?"

And with that, I drop a twenty on the bartop and leave Santa Claus to think about his son.

The one who almost killed me.

## 19

## RAYA

Note to self: when spending the holiday season in Christmas Town, be prepared for Christmas celebrations to begin on December twenty-second.

Actually, the entire village has been abuzz for two nights now, when the annual gingerbread house competition was held.

My creation won second place.

First place? Well, that went to Cassie.

The future Mrs. Claus took the top prize with tears in her eyes and a wobble to her slender, pointy chin. I swear, I heard some of the elves accuse her of cheating. Was there any credence to their claims? I've got no idea, but if anyone would be able to cheat and get away with it? It would be her.

Despite my annoyance that I lost, I kind of feel bad for Cassie. The entire town has forgotten that there will be a wedding in four days.

There is a flour shortage, and none is left to make her wedding cake. Cassie found out the night of the competition, and if Vanilla has the right of it, Cassie cried herself to sleep. I don't know when I started listening to all of the local gossip.

Probably right around the time I realized that I *like* it here.

There's no Vera. No overreaching and perfect shadow. I'm the only Slaski around. I can be my snarky, snappy self and people *love* it. I don't get any *"why can't you be nicer, like your sister"* comments every time I open my mouth.

It's awesome.

The only major downer is the serious lack of intel we've gathered. Even with their flour shortage keeping them busy, Olympus Flour is *not* tied to Vitality Holdings.

"Are you sure?" I ask Jessie for the twentieth time in our two-second conversation on the morning of December twenty-third.

"Yep," she answers, the clickety-clack of her keyboard coming through the line. "They're a family-owned company. They only called themselves Olympus because of an incident at the old flour mill a hundred years ago. There was a huge mountain of flour. They called it Olympus as a joke. It stuck."

"Huh, that's disappointing in a very non-disappointing way."

"Don't feel bad, Raya." A voice comes through the line, and I grit my teeth. "Jack heard from T-Bone that loads of potential leads haven't gone anywhere. The task force exists in an overabundance of caution. There's every chance you won't uncover anything."

"Thanks for that, Vera," I snap through my clenched jaw.

I've been avoiding my sister since I called her drunk off my ass a few nights ago. I have *no* idea what we talked about, nor do I want to know. It's probably not great. Obviously, my brain is a cocktail of embarrassment and shame.

"Oh, sorry about that, Raya," Jessie says. "Forgot to mention your sister is in my office. We're going over some footage that she got of Lisbeth Bannon."

"And did *you uncover anything?*" I'm not asking because I'm rooting for her to fail.

If Vera discovered that Lisbeth Bannon is Hera, Klaus and I would have to leave Christmas Town. I'm not ready for that. I want to stay here a little longer while we figure out what we are to each other. I'm enjoying the protective bubble this strange little village has given me.

"I haven't found a damn thing," she complains dramatically. "Lisbeth went on a holiday last month to Waikiki Beach. Since then? She leads a very boring life. She isn't in contact with anyone shady. She's been focusing on the legitimate side of the business. Vitality. You know, the beauty product line?"

I roll my eyes and mimic her yapping to Klaus, who has been observing our conversation with a grin.

"We're not any closer to figuring out who the hell Hera and Zeus are, then."

"Afraid not," Vera sighs. "But listen. Now that I've got you on the phone..."

"Oh, would you look at that. Klaus is waving me down. Bye. Thanks, Jessie." I hang up and push away from the desk. "Don't you dare say a word."

Klaus can't suppress his smirk. "I've never been so happy that I don't have siblings."

"Be quiet." I flip him off. "I didn't want to have a personal conversation with Vera right there. It wouldn't have been right."

"Sure. That's all."

I want to point out that we've also been avoiding a pretty big topic. *Us.* He doesn't have a leg to stand on.

"What's going to happen to the wreath once we leave? Christmas Town can't have FUC guarding it till the end of time. Eventually, a better solution will have to be found."

"You don't want to be stuck here with me forever?" Klaus jests.

I arch a brow at him. It's a joke, but does he really not understand the implication in his words? "Do *you*?" I test.

"No. Absolutely not."

My shoulders fall despite myself, and he notices. He frowns and comes to stand before me.

"Raya, it's not because of you. I just don't like this town. There's too much pain here. Too many bad memories. We've made some good ones together during our time here, yes. You make Christmas Town better, but we can't stay here forever. We have to go back to reality."

"Right."

Klaus takes my hand in his and pulls me back toward the desk. He motions for me to sit, still holding my hand. "I'm kinda hoping that when we *do* back to FUC, we can keep seeing each other."

I don't move a muscle. I don't blink. I don't even breathe. It's not like I gave him an ultimatum the night we built gingerbread houses at his parents' place, but I hoped he did some thinking about what our connection meant to him. Klaus hasn't brought it up, so I was half expecting it to be a wham-bam-thank-you-ma'am sort of situation.

It would have broken my heart.

"You want to keep seeing me," I repeat for confirmation.

He nods.

"Good. You've come to the right conclusion. I really wouldn't have liked knocking some sense into you."

Klaus laughs softly. "Oh, yeah? And how were you going to do that, exactly?"

"I was going to throw my cranberry lips at you every chance I got. Maybe shimmy out of my leather jacket in tantalizing ways." One of his brows hooks up. "Don't even deny it. I've seen you watch me take it off."

"Guilty. What can I say? You do it for me, Raya."

"Ditto, Blitzy-boo. Super ditto."

He leans over and gives me a sweet kiss. "You're gonna need to come up with a better nickname for me if this is gonna work."

"Not a chance. I like calling you Blitz. It fits."

"Did you know I went by that as a kid?"

I shake my head. *This is it! I will* finally *get the tale of the Blitz.* Easy. Must remain absolutely calm. "No. I literally just shortened the sexiest reindeer name out of the bunch."

"Sexiest?"

I roll my eyes. "Don't even pretend to be a dingus. You *know* I'm into your whole vibe."

"Sorry I didn't catch on right away. I was too mad about having a partner on this mission. Turns out, you're not so bad." Klaus tucks a strand of hair behind my ear. "I don't like it when you call me Blitz because that's what the other kids called me."

I scrunch up my face. "Oh. I apologize, Klaus."

"No. Don't be sorry. You didn't know."

"Why did they call you that?"

Klaus tenses, but as he takes a deep breath, he sits back on the desk. "I was a bit of an odd kid. I didn't like playing with the other children. I preferred spending all of my time with the reindeer. As a Thorsen, I was meant to take over their training one day. It's just what's done for the people in my family."

"I guess training reindeer when you can shift into one makes things a lot easier."

"It sure does. The second I was able to shift I barely ever left them. I don't know why, really. I belonged with them more than with my classmates. They wanted to play workshop and Santa and his deer. I could play with *actual* reindeer."

"Not cops and robbers?"

He chuckles. "No. Niko always played Santa because everyone *knew* he would be Santa one day. It caused a lot of fights between him and Nils. Because I was the only Thorsen and reindeer shifter..." He stops.

"You always had to play the reindeer?"

"Yeah. When I was around eight, a bunch of us kids went up to this small slope near town. We used to slide down on our toboggans there. This one day, Niko decided to push me off the hill."

"What? Why?"

"To see if reindeer shifters could fly. I *obviously* don't. I tumbled down, barreled into a spruce, and flattened it on my fall. I broke my arm."

"Echoing blood bag. That's horrible."

"The other kids banded together and told the adults it was an accident. They were too scared of what Niko would do to *them*. I tried to tell the truth, but no one believed me. No one wanted to hear that their future Santa was a bully."

"That's horrible. Is that why you're scared of heights?"

"No. That came later. After the whole arm incident, *that's* when the kids started calling me Blitz. Because my fall was a swift way to demolish trees. And Niko thought it was very clever because of Blitzen."

"What a little dick."

Klaus shrugs.

"I had no idea. I won't call you that anymore."

"You know what? Don't stop calling me Blitz. I like that

you're rewriting what it means. Just like you're changing what it feels like to be in this town."

"It can mean that you demolish my underwear," I add with a wink.

He laughs softly. "Sure. I like that."

"I'm really sorry you went through such a rough time."

"It wasn't the end."

I winced. "Figured."

"Our senior year in high school, I went through a growth spurt. All of a sudden, I was taller and bigger than Niko. I made it pretty damn obvious that I wouldn't stand for his bullshit anymore. He didn't like that."

"Of course he didn't. I really don't think this douchebucket should be Santa."

"You and me both. It should be Nils."

"It should be, yeah. What happened with Niko?"

"We hiked up a mountain a few miles out of town. It was supposed to be a toboggan race challenge."

"Clearly the only way to resolve anything in Christmas Town."

"Exactly. We got to the top, and obviously, being two dumb seventeen-year-olds, we started talking smack. I told Niko that Nils was a better Santa. Some other really shitty stuff too. He got mad and threw me off the mountain."

I gasp and reach out for his hand.

"This time, it wasn't a little hill. It was a *mountain*. I broke a few limbs. Had a concussion, too. Probably would've died if I wasn't a shifter."

"If you tell me it was deemed an accident, I'm gonna..."

Klaus gives me a small smile. It's so sad and heavy my heart nearly breaks for him. "He claimed it was an accident. There were no witnesses, and though Nils tried to speak out for me, once again, no one believed me. As soon as I graduated high school, I left."

I am speechless. I am a lot of things. "No one thought it was weird?"

"I wasn't exactly liked in town. I was the weird reindeer kid. They all wanted to believe Niko wasn't... *isn't...* a piece of shit."

"They literally made you Rudolph. Do they not see that?"

"I don't think so."

"You know what, Klaus? We are going to save this town, and then? I'm gonna give 'em a piece of my mind." I seal my words with a kiss because I *mean* it.

I might be a vampire bat with a serial killer aunt, but I'm going to teach the land of joy and giving a thing or two about kindness.

## 20

## KLAUS

It's the blizzard of the century.

Or so everyone in town is claiming.

Let's forget for a second that Christmas Town is in the north. It snows here. A lot. Yet somehow, every time there's going to be a good dumping of snow, everyone panics. Especially when it's the day before Christmas Eve *and* there's a wedding in three days.

Every elf is bustling around town like their lives depend on it. There's baking, last-minute toy-making, frantic gift wrapping. Tape is running low, but the real tragedy is that there is an actual flour shortage.

The Olympus Flour truck meant to deliver the last of the flour for belated Christmas baking, *and* the wedding cake, is nowhere to be seen. Apparently, it's been delayed due to inclement weather.

Because their truck isn't basically a tank.

Cassie is a mess. Niko is trying to convince everyone in town to pool their flour to make the wedding cake. Doris is trying to keep the peace while Santa is doing what he does:

getting the deliveries ready. My parents are with the rein-deer, making sure they're ready for the Christmas rush.

That leaves Raya and me alone in the security office, watching the now locked glass case. After we spotted Santa picking the wreath out of its secure spot, we upped security. The glass is bulletproof, and Raya has the only key hidden in her sexy-as-fuck combat boot.

Santa can try to pull the wool over my eyes with all of his faith bullshit.

I don't buy it.

He's still letting his almost-murderous psycho son take up the Santa mantle once he retires. If Nils decided to enlist Vitality Holdings to help him get rid of his brother, I don't even know if I would blame him. The thought makes me uncomfortable as hell.

"Officer Wassail Sugarplum will be here shortly to take over the afternoon shift. He'll do a couple of hours for us while we get an early dinner. I figured he'd want to be with his wife and kids later on."

I grin at Raya's thoughtfulness. Funny how it's an outsider that brings the joy and kindness Christmas Town is supposed to naturally have.

"That was really sweet of you."

"Don't thank me yet. We're making it up to your parents by having dinner with them on the twenty-sixth. We'll cele-brate Christmas on our terms, on our schedule this year. So what if it's a little later."

"Good idea."

Raya's jaw drops. "Are you kidding? That's it? I thought this would be a big blowout fight."

"Nope. It's nice. I'm sure you made my parents very happy."

"Stop. Hardly."

*You've made me the happiest I've ever been.*

But I don't say that. It's too much, too soon. Maybe one day, I'll tell Raya what she means to me. One thing is clear. I do care for her. She is the only person who knows the truth of my history here.

I trust her *that* much.

---

Officer Wassail Sugarplum relieves us of our guard duties for a little while, which is just as well. I'm *starving* and totally jonesing for a massive slice of tourtière slathered in ketchup. We stop in at one of the small restaurants, Scrumptious Joy.

The whole town is in a state of pure panic because of the storm. We eat from our seats at the massive window and watch as large, fluffy flakes fall from the sky.

It's too beautiful to make me dread the steady fall. Sure, if this pace kept up, soon the entire town will be covered in a foot of heavy snow. We are ready for it. It's not like it's an unusual occurrence.

"This is so beautiful," Raya whispers, mesmerized by the snow.

I'm captivated by *her*. "Did you get much snow where you grew up?"

"Some. Nothing like this. This one year, when we were little, Vera and I built this huge fort. It wasn't *that* big, but it felt ginormous for us. We spent hours in there, playing make-believe. It was so fun. I remember begging my parents to let us play some more, even though we were turning into tiny ice cubes."

"That's a nice memory."

She smiles. "Yeah. It is. I honestly forgot about it until just now."

"You used to get along with Vera, then."

Raya sighs with a heavy shrug. "We did, yeah. Actually, we were *really* close when we were itty-bitty bats. It's once she started school that things took a turn. She was a natural student, and I was most assuredly *not*. I don't know who made the comparison first, but it doesn't matter. What matters is that it stuck. It got roped into the whole family dynamic."

"I'm really sorry about that."

She waves me off. "It's nothing. Sibling rivalry isn't that interesting."

I lean over the table to brush my fingers against her cheek. "I don't know about that. We're in a town where sibling rivalry is pretty damn important. It dictates the whole future of this place."

"I guess that's true."

"Do you think you'll ever be close to Vera again?"

She scrunches up her face. "I don't know. I called her when we got drunk. I've got no clue what I said to her."

"Really? I think, deep down, you know."

She points her fork at me before stealing a bite of my tourtière. "Don't you try to analyze me, mister."

"Fair enough." The silence stretches on between us as I wait to see if she'll get it off her chest.

Raya clicks her tongue and rolls her eyes. "I *might* have apologized for being so competitive. And *maybe* I took ownership for my own actions. But I don't want to talk about it anymore. I get all cringy when I think about it too hard. Let's drop it?"

"Yup. Dropping it." I peek at my watch, and a plan takes hold of my mind. "Hey, I wanna show you something." I drop a few bills on the table to pay for our meal and tow Raya across the street and all the way to the reindeer training center.

It's the place where my father and all of my ancestors have worked for generations now. It's where I would work if things had turned out differently for me.

I show Raya around, introducing her to the reindeer. I don't know them by name anymore, but being a reindeer myself, the beautiful animals take to me quite easily.

I show Raya how to saddle them to the sleigh. She's especially taken by a reindeer named Stockings. He's a silly one, barely able to contain his excitement at going for a ride.

"I've missed this. Being around the reindeer like this. Forgot how peaceful it is to just be here, in the barn."

"Probably why you prefer working alone."

I chuckle softly. "You're right."

"You liked it, didn't you? Working here? If things had been different, had things not gone sideways with Niko?"

I sigh as the validity of her words settles into me. "Yeah. I think so."

"It's not too late," she whispers.

"Sure it is. Niko is about to get married. He'll take over the town. I'm not living under his thumb, training *his* reindeer. Not a Grinch's chance in Whoville is that happening."

*Now, if* Nils *were to be in charge...* I shake my head, hoping to chase away the thought.

Sensing the shift in my mood, Raya changes the subject. "What exactly are we doing? We need to take over for Officer Sugarplum in two hours."

"We'll be back in time." I help her up into the sleigh and tuck a thick red plaid blanket across her knees. "We really need to get you better winter clothes next time we come here."

"Next time, huh?"

"Don't bust my balls about this, Raya."

"Oh, fine. Be that way." She smirks at me, pleased at my slip-up.

In truth, I think I'm planning a whole lifetime of Christmases with Raya. After only a couple of weeks as her partner, that should be *insane*.

It's not.

My parents were engaged after a month, married after two, and I was already on the way somewhere in between.

I've got a feeling deep in my heart that it'll be similar for us.

"It's Christmas Eve-Eve. This town gets a little nutso this time of the holiday season."

Raya throws her head back with a giggle. "A little nutso? We've officially been spending a lot of time together."

A small smile tugs at my lips. "Maybe." I place a soft kiss on her lips.

Two weeks ago, if someone would have told me that I'd be in my hometown with a batty lady I was *definitely* falling for during Christmas time? I would have laughed myself silly.

Yet here it is.

"Are you going to tell me where we're going?"

"I'm taking you to the very edge of town."

"Sweet suffering mammal. Are you bringing me to *the* mountain?"

"Sure am."

"But why?"

"I wanna make a new memory there. One that's all roped up in you."

"Wow. That's a good line, Blitzy-boo."

"Not a line if I mean it."

Raya folds her arm under mine, laying her head on my shoulder as we slide over the thick snow with more of it steadily falling over us. The ride takes only about fifteen minutes on a good day, but after twenty minutes, the mountaintop comes into view over a bushy line of spruce trees. I pull the sleigh to a stop and lean back into my seat to let the peace settle into my soul.

"Damn. I've missed this place."

"It actually suits you. You're so much calmer here. I mean don't get me wrong. You're still *way* grumpy, but it's different. You're more…" She chews her lower lip, thinking for the right word. "Settled. You seem more settled."

"Thanks, Raya. That means a lot to me, actually." I kiss her softly, and it's just as I'm pulling away that I spot it.

A huge light blue truck with the words Olympus Flour painted on the side.

That's not what makes my blood run cold.

Nope.

It's the four busted tires.

## 21

## RAYA

*Craptastic tinsel bombs!*

"No fucking way," I gasp. "Is that the missing flour shipment?"

"We need to get back to town. *Now*," Klaus roars. "I'm not gonna make the reindeer haul our asses back to town. I'll get them to make their way back safely without us. We need to shift."

"On it," I blurt out, preparing myself for the change. "I'll have to stay close to you. Can't freeze to death before we even get to the good stuff."

He nods. "Destination is the wreath."

"You got it, Blitz."

I wish I could watch Klaus turn into the majestic reindeer that he is, but I'm too busy becoming a one-ounce bat. It doesn't hurt, exactly. It doesn't feel good, either. It's sort of like really bad period cramps when my uterus is basically trying to escape my body to get the hell away from the hormones coursing through my veins.

Like that, only a million times worse.

Thankfully, it only lasts a few moments.

Klaus is through his shift. His coat is a thick, shiny chocolate brown on which snowflakes melt. His antlers are a fuzzy crown of badassery. He can do some serious damage with those. His eyes, usually beautiful emerald green, are now dark green. He groans and moves his head, motioning for me to hop on.

I do. I latch onto one of his antlers, perching there like a bird.

I'd fly if it wasn't snowing like the sky was falling. The wind is so strong it's likely to send me twenty feet in the wrong direction. With me settled onto him, Klaus books it and squalls to the reindeer. The animals don't seem overly concerned but begin to follow in our footsteps at a leisurely pace. We soon outrun them.

The sleigh ride took us about twenty minutes, but Klaus manages to get us into town in half that time. The snow-covered streets aren't deserted. A few courageous souls brave the weather to get last-minute errands in. They don't even see us running by through the wall of flakes covering the town.

This is bad.

I don't know *why* the Olympus Flour truck is in the middle of nowhere with busted-out tires, but it's hardly a good sign.

It basically spells disaster if disaster is spelled Hera and Zeus.

Or Vitality Holdings.

Klaus doesn't stop once we've reached Santa's workshop. I sense what he's about to do and take off, flapping my wings in the frigid wind. Klaus rams his antlers into the doors, forcing them open. As soon as there is a crack, I fly through. It takes him a few more tries to make his way in, but when he does, he quickly catches up.

We run by the cabooses, not bothering to hop on. Our shifter bodies are way more convenient. There isn't a single elf in sight. I wish I knew if it was normal. You'd think that there would be a few here and there, making a few things, wrapping a couple of toys for the kids who changed sides of that dreaded list at the last minute.

"Would you just *break* it?" A shrill voice echoes through the long hall.

"No," a second sniffling response comes.

"You're *useless.* I won't let a full life's work go to waste because of *you.*"

I fly with everything I have. I move my wings faster than is safe, but I need to know who is in Santa's office.

We finally come within sight of it, and honestly? It's not what I expected.

A young woman with shiny blonde curls and a freckled face is wiping a steady stream of tears while Vanilla shouts at her, her starched lace bonnet flopping precariously on top of her head.

*What the damn hell is going on?*

Knowing this will need at least *one* agent in human form to communicate, I shift back.

"Stop right there."

The blonde covers her eyes with a squeak, no doubt surprised by my blatant nudity. Vanilla blanches, turning the color of her bonnet.

"Raya, hey there. I thought you were gone." She tries to appear calm but fails. Her entire body is shaking.

"I came back. What's going on here?" I aim my question to the trembling young woman. "Are you okay? Cookie, right? You're Cookie Trimmings?"

She hiccups a sob and nods. "Yes."

I grab one of the thick throws from one of the chairs and

wrap it around me. "Better?" I ask her. Seriously. It's only a naked body. What's her deal? Humans are funny about stuff like that.

Cookie takes a step toward me, clearly desperate to get away from Vanilla. "Help," she mouths.

Klaus, now back to his sexy man-self, takes another throw and hides his dangly bits. "Vanilla, please tell me you're not trying to steal the wreath."

The older woman throws her hands up. "For Rudolph's sake. Of course not!"

I am shocked. Truly. Vanilla is barely four feet tall. She is close to a hundred if she's any age at all. She's Santa's head elf *and* her family has worked in the workshop for *generations*. She told me so herself the very first day I met her. It seemed to be such a point of pride.

"Frankincense," she bellows. "Get your figgy pudding in here."

The blubbering elf, the one who went on holiday to Hawaii—the one we *cleared*—sheepishly walks in, holding a gun.

"Where's Officer Sugarplum?" I growl. I stalk toward him, only to realize the weapon is a toy.

Go figure.

"He's fine, the big lug. We slipped a bit too much booze in his White Christmas. He's snoring at the security desk," Vanilla explains. "What gave us away?"

"Honestly?" Klaus answers. "Nothing. I didn't suspect you at all. We just found the flour truck."

Vanilla rolls her eyes. "I told you we needed to do a better job at hiding that damn thing."

"Where's the driver?" Klaus takes the question right out of my mouth.

"Back at our place. Safe and sound, if a little wrapped up," Vanilla grumbles.

"Holy holly balls," I exclaim. "I know what happened."

"Please," Klaus grumbles. "Enlighten me because I'm so confused right now."

"It's actually super simple. I should have figured it out the *second* I learned that Lisbeth Bannon was in Waikiki Beach. That's in Hawaii. She wasn't on holiday. She was meeting Frankincense. Probably to edge her out of Vitality Holdings after she got caught with the whole Val Downer thing."

"Umm, Raya? Still lost here. Lead me to it, would ya, sweets?"

"Vanilla is Hera. Frankincense is Zeus. *They're* behind Vitality Holdings. I'm guessing they put all of Christmas Town's equity in funding their chase for immortality."

"Please tell me she's wrong," Klaus shouts. "You didn't, Vanilla. You love this place."

"Exactly! I love this place. I would do *anything* for this town. Ever since Santa had his two sons, I've known I would have to step up to the plate and save this town. Everyone assumed that Niko would take the throne, so to speak. I know he's a bad egg. I'm one of the only people in town who saw that lunatic for what he is. He's one donkey short of a manger scene. You should know that, Klaus."

"Of course I do. Why didn't you ever say anything?" he asks.

"Oh," she snorts dryly. "I did. I did. Every day, I was in Nik's ear about his oldest. He wouldn't hear of it. The more I pushed, the more he threatened to replace me. Nils would be such a better choice. I was so excited when Nils was with this one." She juts her chin in Cookie's direction. "I thought they would get married. Then the dolt went and broke up with Nils, leaving the Santa role wide open for Niko."

"I didn't have a choice," Cookie interjects between two sobs. "Niko and Cassie made me do it."

"Fuck me." Klaus runs a hand over his face.

"Well, I didn't know *that*," Vanilla screams. "That would've been good information to have."

"They're not even *together*. He hired her to play his fiancée," Cookie continues.

"Of all the devious bullshit," I say in complete disbelief.

"I knew he was bad news, but this takes the cake. Seriously, Vanilla. You tried to use the Bloody Doctor's research to find immortality? You blackmailed a FUC agent with death?"

"Frankincense is great with all that stuff. He's not just a cook and baker but a bit of a scientist, too. We needed the proper leverage. We need our current Santa to live forever. We can't ever get so close to losing Christmas Town to a demonic spawn like Niko."

I want to point out that she and her husband have been pretty demonic themselves, but I refrain. It's hard to do, but I really don't need to add fuel to the fire.

"And when the Bloody Doctor *and* the Vitality people failed, you what? Started to believe in the magic of the wreath?"

"Oh." Vanilla laughs. "We weren't *after* the wreath at all. That thing has no power. We wanted to break into the safe and steal some of the money. A lot of it is missing already. I had to pay goons to do our busy work. It's not like we could leave town. That would've been too suspicious."

"So Klaus and I being here for the wreath was, what? Just a bad coincidence?"

Vanilla snorts. "Yup. We were going to frame Cassie for

the missing cash tonight. Cookie tried to stop us. She wanted us to come clean to you. Said you could help."

"We could've," Klaus insists.

The elf pouts. "I was trying to avoid jail time. I was hoping to pin the whole thing on Cassie. It would've been fine by me, given that we've been trying to sabotage the wedding all week."

"Hence the flour shortage." I nod. "You weren't merely delivering cookies, were you, Frankincense? You were stashing flour."

The elf blushes with shame. "I'm just trying to save something bigger than myself."

"Yeah, well, you went about it all wrong. More secrecy and lies, more hurt and deceit doesn't do shit. That's like trying to fix a sinking ship with modeling clay." I shake my head, still reeling from this strange revelation. And I thought my sister's first case with a pumpkin-shifting botanist was intense.

"You do realize you'll be charged with a whole bunch of crimes, right?" Klaus asks Vanilla and Frankincense.

"So long as you promise not to let Niko take over, I don't care," the elf states, putting out her arms to be handcuffed. "Frankincense, come on. Time to pay the piper."

The elf's eyes are full of sadness. "Tradition is so important, you know? It's not that we didn't want things to change. We just got so scared that Niko would burn it all down. He's a bad man. He doesn't stand for love and community. He's only after himself. That's not what this town was ever about."

Too bad they didn't speak out all those years ago when Klaus was only a little boy.

More than one life could have been saved, then.

ONCE WE GET the big man back to the workshop, pulling him away from his pre-delivery nap, it takes Klaus and me a little while to explain everything. He and Doris listen to every word, more and more horrified.

"Nils will have to take over, obviously. As soon as possible, too. It's clear to me now that I am no longer fit to wear the suit. I've got to step down."

Doris sniffs and dabs at her eyes. "How did we go so wrong with him?"

I wish I had the answer for her. I really do. "Nils is a sweet man. I'm sure he'll do a great job at upholding traditions, all the while breathing new life into town."

"I think Nils should be brought here," Klaus adds. "I'm pretty sure this young lady will want to have a nice long chat with him."

Cookie gives him a grateful smile. "I never stopped loving him. I was so scared that Niko would hurt Nils or me. The whole town, really. He said he'd burn my shop down if I spoke a word. Nils warned me about him. About what he was capable of. I thought if I played nice..." She wipes a few stray tears from her cheeks. "I thought it would work out in the end."

"It will," I cut in. "Things can work out if everyone does their part to *make* it a better place."

Hours later, well into the morning of Christmas Eve, Vanilla, Frankincense, Lisbeth Bannon, and a few other goons are arrested. Cassie is revealed for the fraud that she is, while Niko has been permanently banned from his hometown.

That seems too easy a punishment, but he's a slick

bastard. He hasn't done anything illegal. Too bad being a major selfish jackass isn't a crime.

Everyone in Christmas Town knows that, tonight, a new Santa will sit in the sleigh.

Nils.

And by his side, his future wife, Cookie.

# EPILOGUE


One Year Later

Christmas Eve at the Thorsen house is a little bit hectic but in the best way possible. It's the kind of chaos that fills your heart with so much joy and happiness it could burst.

One year ago, if someone would've told me that I'd be married to a reindeer trainer, living in Christmas Town as the posted FUC agent? I would've laughed myself silly.

That's exactly what happened.

Once Niko was exiled, Vanilla, Frankincense, and their accomplices were arrested, and Nils became the new and much improved Santa, the threat to the wreath stopped.

The possibilities of people chasing immortality also very much decreased.

Yet, somehow, Director Cooper decided it would be a good idea to have a permanent FUC agent in Christmas Town, working in conjunction with CTPD.

I took the job in a heartbeat. It helped that Klaus wanted to stay.

That's right. Klaus I'm-angry-at-the-world-and-hate-Christmas Thorsen wanted to move back to his hometown. He's been working with his father, training reindeer. Honestly, I've never seen my man-bun god happier.

This is where he belongs. He got lost there for a while, but he found his place.

As did I.

All I've ever wanted was a place to call my own. A place where I could stand out and be my own person with no one's shadow or reputation making me feel small. I have that here, in Christmas Town.

The small house Klaus and I own on the outskirts of the village is packed today. Not only are Nils and Cookie here for a quick visit before getting ready for the big delivery, but we're hosting a whole lot of people.

My in-laws, Holly and Patridge, are here.

So are my parents and extended family.

Mila, my uncle, T-Bone, Bettina, and baby Courtney Thrussel IV, better known as Baby T, are here. Though I've warned everyone that the poor kid will need a better nick-name down the line, he is downright the cutest, pudgiest little boy I've ever seen. Even at barely a month old, he is a heartbreaker.

Vera and her husband, Jack, are here, too. They got married a couple of months before Klaus and me. Not that there was any sort of competition.

I'm *really* working hard on that. I'm better. I think it helps that I'm on my own turf in Christmas Town, while Vera does all kinds of surveillance stuff for FUC.

It's funny, really. Three vampire bats, adverse to the sun and reliant on blood to live, and we found our happily ever after with the Furry United Coalition.

All different, yet all with one common goal: to leave the world better than how we found it.

That's basically my life motto now.

It's also how I plan to raise my kids. I'm about four months away if my due date is accurate. Announcing it to both our families at the same time so close to Christmas is the best gift ever.

The long table, made up of smaller tables pulled together, runs from our living room to the dining room. The din is loud but happy. Sitting to my right, Klaus brings my hand up to his mouth and kisses my knuckles.

"You ready?" he whispers.

"Yup." I give him a wink before standing. I clink a knife to my glass and wait for the conversations to die down. "I'm so happy that everyone I care about is gathered here right now. This is what this time of the year is all about. Family, whether related or found." Cookie beams at me. "We'll need a new place setting next time we all gather." I pat my stomach. "We're expecting a little bundle of screams—er, I mean *joy*—soon enough."

Mom gasps and bursts into tears, and Dad pats her back, repeating over and over that he's so proud of his daughters for building happy lives for themselves. Vera congratulates me with flushed cheeks and a watery smile.

"Vera?" I ask. "Are you okay?"

She waves me off. "Yes, of course. I'm so happy for you both."

I arch a brow. "You wanna share something with the rest of the class?"

"No, no. I couldn't."

I make my way around the table and tug her to her feet. "Seriously, it's okay." I grin at her because I mean it. It's not about competition or comparison. It's about the joy of sharing life's beautiful moments.

"You're sure?"

I nod, and she grips my hand.

"Well," she begins, smirking at Jack, "we're also having a baby."

The room explodes in another round of cheers, but I hold my sister tight. We might have been caught up in rivalry. We might even live a world apart now. That doesn't matter. She's my sister, and though she drives me nutso bananas sometimes, I love her. More than that, I would *choose* her as a sister.

"Bats are gonna take over Christmas Town," Mila roars. "I love this for us. We're FUC's very merry band of bats, spreading the batty message far and wide."

"Sweet suffering mammal." Cookie giggles, borrowing my favorite expression. "What does the future hold?"

"Hope," I answer, my hand going to the barely noticeable bump at my stomach. "The future holds hope."

Klaus winks at me from his seat, and I soak it all up.

Love, hope, family. And I know, down to the core of my soul, that this happily ever after? It's not just mine. It's *ours*. From the bats to the reindeer to Hairy Coo and the exploding pumpkin. We might be a ragtag bunch, but we fit together.

**The End.**

*Or is it?* There are more FUC Academy books from other authors coming your way soon!

To find out more about these books and more, visit worlds.EveLanglais.com or sign up for the EveL Worlds newsletter. If you haven't already downloaded the **free Academy intro** (written by Eve Langlais) make sure you grab it at

worlds.evelanglais.com/wordpress/book/fucacademy1!

*This bat likes a good bone...*

Mila Starling is a forensic anthropologist who studies bones. And as a vampire bat, she loves her steak raw but her Highland cattle shifter detectives hot.

The last thing that Mila ever expected was for The Bloody Doctor to escape prison after nearly two decades of incarceration. But Detective T-Bone, a tall wall of muscular man cake, drops the bomb that the notorious serial killer is on the loose. He's come to enlist Mila's help due to her encyclopedic knowledge of the notorious serial killer's crimes.

Too bad he didn't realize that Mila's obsession with the atrocities was the daughter trying to make up for the sins of the mother. That's right. T-Bone's new partner is the murderer's daughter. But Mila is adamant that her link to the Bloody Doctor won't stop her from bringing her mother to justice. They head out on the road, hoping to catch their mark before more bodies pile up. Their mission brings them to the Bloody Doctor's jail cell where the proof is in the blood.

**Out now on all platforms!**

# BAT AND THE JACK

*Must love blood? Not quite.*

Vera Slaski might be a vampire bat, but she's got a secret. She cannot stand the sight of blood. She managed to keep that hidden for a long time. She's seconds away from becoming a full-blown FUC agent when she is exposed.

To regain Director Cooper's trust and finally earn her badge, Vera is sent on a bona fide babysitting mission. All she has to do is keep a key witness safe and make sure no blood is shed—for her own sake.

When Vera arrives at the secluded cabin in the woods, the last thing she expects is a massive pumpkin where Dr. Norbert Palomer should be. Then the gourd explodes. Literally.

With the mad botanist's secret revealed, Vera realizes the mission won't be a prance through the garden. There are some bad people out there who will stop at nothing to get their hands on the experiment gone oh-so wrong.

Between a vampire bat who can't drink blood and a scientist who shifts into a jack-o'-lantern, the odds of survival don't look great.

But FUC is on the case, and this bat? She's bent on flying the roost and straight into the pumpkin patch.

**Out now on all platforms!**

# ABOUT THE AUTHOR

A. Gregory writes magically delicious stories that will transport you to the places where things go bump in the night. Sometimes there's magic, other times there are shifters, but there is always a happily ever after.

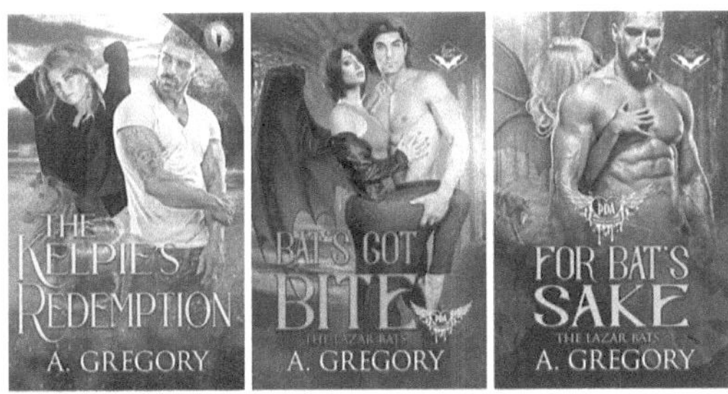

instagram.com/a.gregory.paranormal

9 798201 965150